A Capital Christmas

by

Sarah Hendess

Christmas in the Castle

The Wild Rose Press, Inc.
PO Box 708
Adams Basin, NY 14410-0708
Visit us at www.thewildrosepress.com

Publishing History
First Edition, 2024
Trade Paperback ISBN 978-1-5092-5645-7
Digital ISBN 978-1-5092-5646-4

Christmas in the Castle
Published in the United States of America

Dedication

For my oldest friend, Nicole,
who's always stood by me,
even when I've done something stupid.

A Note on Language

Members of the Religious Society of Friends ("Quakers" or simply "Friends") originally used "plain speech." When Quakerism emerged in England in the mid-1600s, the word "you" was not used as a singular pronoun as it is today. "Thee" and "thou" were used to address a single person, and "you" was used for groups of two or more *or* when addressing a social superior, such as a member of the peerage. Because Quakers believe in the equality of all persons, they refused to use the deferential "you" to social superiors, using "thee" and "thou" regardless of to whom they were speaking. They also refused to use titles, even "Mr." and "Miss," preferring instead to refer to people by either their first or their first *and* last names, regardless of their social station. This brought them a great deal of ire and persecution from the people in power, causing many Quakers to seek refuge in America. By the mid-nineteenth century, for simplicity's sake, they'd dropped "thou" and used "thee" ("thee does" instead of "thou dost") in all instances.

Though it may rankle the strict grammarian, Caleb Fox speaks this way throughout the book to stay true to the time period. Also in line with Quakers of the time, Caleb refers to the days of the week by their number rather than by their common names, which are largely derived from the names of pagan gods. By the mid-twentieth century, plain speech had mostly died out, though Quakers' commitment to integrity and simplicity keeps a certain type of plain speech alive by encouraging Friends to be clear and direct with their words.

Chapter One

Washington City, District of Columbia
October 20, 1859

Fiona had to remind herself that Nicole was only getting married, not dying. But it was a struggle. After two years of Fiona's being the only female employee at the Smithsonian Institution, Nicole's arrival had seemed to herald a new era in which women commonly worked in the professions.

The professions that allowed women to remain on their *feet*, anyway, Fiona thought. There were plenty of working women in the city. Poor, desperate creatures who staved off starvation only by catering to the baser desires of the politicians.

Fiona shook her head. No employer let a man go once he wed. If her colleague were "Nicholas" instead of "Nicole," the marriage next month would change nothing. "Nicholas" would be absent from work for a few days and then carry on as usual. Instead, Fiona stared down the barrel of once again being the sole paid female employee at the Institution—a lone woman adrift in a sea of men.

She sighed. She should be happy for her friend, regardless of the marriage's deleterious effect on Nicole's employment. And she supposed she was. The joy on Nicole's face every time she mentioned David was infectious, and ultimately, Fiona wanted nothing more than for her friend to be happy.

One thing was certain, though: she herself was *never* getting married. Not when it would spell the end of her career. And at thirty years old, she was long considered an old maid, so no one pressed her about it.

Approaching footsteps echoed through the cavernous library, and Fiona looked up from the catalog she was updating. A dark-haired man, perhaps a few years older than herself, ambled in her direction. He gazed wide-eyed up at the soaring groin-vaulted ceiling and nearly tripped over a table where a Columbian College professor sat studying a map of Roman Gaul.

She shook her head again, but this time she smiled. Nestled in the West Wing of the Smithsonian Institution—the "Castle" as Washingtonians had taken to calling it—the library often awed first-time visitors. Designed to mimic the collegiate buildings of medieval England, the Castle's deep-red sandstone stood in stark contrast to the white, classical shapes of the capital's other government buildings. The whole structure felt solid and impregnable. If anyone ever invaded Washington City like the British had in 1814, Fiona would hide out here. And given the recent tensions in town over John Brown's attack on Harpers Ferry a few days ago, someone just might.

"May I help you, sir?" she said when the gentleman finally reached her desk.

She noticed immediately that while his frock coat was clean and neat and made of fine black wool, it was of simple design with plain wooden buttons rather than the fashionable shiny brass. His coat hung open, revealing a plain gray vest—again, well-made but utterly unlike the flashy, bright patterns the politicians in Washington favored. The black, broad-brimmed hat he held under his arm was simple as well, its crown several inches shorter than was popular.

Laughter bubbled up from Fiona's belly. Six years in Washington and she'd finally met a man who wasn't fussy about his wardrobe. She hadn't known such men even existed in this town. Even her dear brother George, God rest his soul, had been a dandy.

Before it escaped, though, her laughter faded on her lips when she met this man's gaze. Locks of dark hair fell over his forehead, nearly brushing his thick, dark brows. Beneath a beautifully sculpted nose, his full lower lip gave way to a strong, clean-shaven chin.

But his eyes were what truly captivated her. He had the most vibrant green eyes she'd ever seen, and she couldn't tear her gaze away.

"Pardon me," he said, those brilliant emerald eyes widening but never leaving hers. "I wish to consult with a librarian."

Fiona beamed. "You have found one." She extended her right hand. "Miss Fiona Ellicott, director of the Smithsonian Institution Library, at your service."

The man's eyes widened even further. He didn't seem to notice Fiona's outstretched hand.

"Thee is in charge of," he swept a hand, indicating the entire West Wing, "all *this*?"

Fiona's first instinct was to be annoyed. She'd headed up the library for more than a year now, ever since George had succumbed to a fever, leaving the directorship vacant. She'd been in charge of creating the library catalog, so Secretary Clark had simply promoted her upon George's death. George had trained her well, and she was every bit as capable at running this library as any man would be. Why did every man who came in feel compelled to express indignation when they encountered her?

She narrowed her eyes, ready to show this gentleman just how in charge of this library she was, when she got a better look at the expression on his face. He was surprised by her declaration, certainly, but not offended. Indeed, he looked...*delighted*. Fiona couldn't help smiling back.

"That is truly astounding," the man said, finally noticing and clasping her hand in both of his. His palms were warm and rough, as if he knew hard work. But he didn't strike her as a farmer, and Fiona wondered which profession he pursued. "It is past time the government recognized the equal worth of women."

Fiona rocked back on her heels. Who *was* this man? She had to pause a moment before she could reply. "I am inclined to agree with you, Mr....?"

"Apologies," the man said, releasing her hand, which immediately cooled for want of his skin against hers. "Fox. Caleb Fox. I'm the director of the Friends' Home School in Georgetown."

"The orphanage?" She'd heard of the Friends' Home. The Religious Society of Friends had opened it only a few years ago to rescue street children from the Poor and Work House of Georgetown, where they were essentially incarcerated alongside petty thieves, drunkards, fallen women, and paupers. An appalling situation, to be sure, especially next door to the nation's capital. But the well-fed men of Congress didn't seem to care a fig for the homeless children who swarmed the city, and Fiona was grateful that the Friends had stepped in.

Mr. Fox nodded. "I'm both the director and the head teacher there." He brushed a lock of hair from his forehead and smiled, clearly proud of his position, and Fiona lost track of herself for a moment, admiring his features again. He stared right back at her, and Fiona felt a flicker of something pass between them.

The echo of a chair scraping across the floor on the other side of the library snapped her back to the task at hand.

"Well, Mr. Fox, director and head teacher of the Friends' Home School, how might I assist you?"

She wouldn't have thought it possible, but Mr. Fox grinned even more broadly at her question. And she couldn't be sure—the library's lighting was uneven at best—but she thought perhaps his cheeks reddened a bit.

He explained that he hoped to bring the children— there were only twelve of them, all old enough to attend school—to see the exhibits at the Smithsonian and had come over from Georgetown to scout it out. He'd arrived a couple hours ago and had wandered through the East Wing and the main hall before ending his exploration here in the library.

"I fear we'll have to skip the Laboratory of Natural History," he said. "Some of the children have weak lungs, and the odor there…"

Fiona laughed. "Is pungent," she said. "And the specimens tend to attract fleas, so you're wise to give it a wide berth." Secretary Clark's living quarters were on the floor above the lab in the East Wing, and he and his wife were forever lamenting the horrible odor wafting up into their rooms. "But I expect the children will enjoy the main hall. The exhibits there are quite popular with guests. Children especially enjoy the taxidermied birds."

Behind her, Nicole let out an audible shudder, and Fiona laughed again. She hadn't realized her colleague had come to the desk—Nicole must have finished her reshelving—or she wouldn't have mentioned the birds. The stuffed birds with their glass eyes terrified Nicole so much she wouldn't walk past them, even in broad daylight and when the exhibit hall was full of visitors. Fiona asked her once why they bothered her so, and Nicole managed only a few sputtered phrases about her grandmother's rooster before she asked Fiona not to speak of it again.

Mr. Fox chuckled. "I shall certainly bring them to view the specimens. I am certain they would quite enjoy seeing this magnificent library as well." His eyes widened. "If thee is agreeable, of course."

She smiled at his use of "thee." The word alone should have helped her identify him as a Quaker before he ever mentioned his vocation. That explained his plain clothing too. She'd always thought the Quakers' use of the old terms was affected, but coming from this man, it was downright charming.

"I would be delighted to show the children around our collection," she said. Some of their regular patrons might be less than delighted to see a herd of children descend on the library, but that was their problem, Fiona supposed. The local professors and lawmen could survive being inconvenienced for an hour or two.

"Wonderful," Mr. Fox said. "Would next week be all right? Perhaps Fourth Day?"

Fiona paused. She knew the Quakers referred to the days of the week by number rather than name, and she had to count the days in her head to be sure she knew which one Mr. Fox meant. "Yes, Wednesday would work just fine."

"Wonderful," Mr. Fox said again. "Until then, might I trouble thee to help me find some information about George Washington? I'm preparing a lesson. I'd hoped to take the children to see Mount Vernon, but I fear the estate is about to return to the earth. It would likely discourage the children more than inspire them."

Fiona nodded knowingly. Her brother had taken her to Mount Vernon a few years ago, and the mansion was nearly falling in on itself then. It was a miracle the place was still standing. Hopefully the newly formed Mount Vernon Ladies Association would be able to restore it, since the government clearly had no interest in preserving the home of its first president.

"I know just the book." She slipped from behind the desk and beckoned for Mr. Fox to follow her.

She led him across the library, his footsteps echoing behind her as they crossed the cavernous space. When they reached a bank of shelves, she slipped between two of them and paused about halfway down the aisle and unlocked the glass door on the front of the shelf. She searched only a moment before her fingers landed on the volume she was after. She pulled the leatherbound book off the shelf and coughed as a cloud of dust puffed up. How the books managed to get dusty even behind glass, she'd never understand.

"Please, allow me," Mr. Fox said. He took the book and pulled a handkerchief out of his pocket. Fiona caught a glimpse of a brightly embroidered monogram before Mr. Fox's eyes widened and he slipped the handkerchief back in his pocket. He shifted the book to his other hand and dug into his other pocket, extracting a plain, white square of cotton. He wiped off the book and handed it back to Fiona, not meeting her eyes as he slipped his now dusty handkerchief back into his pocket.

That was strange, but Fiona was used to encountering odd patrons. Oddity was a common ailment among scholars. She shrugged and took the book. Leading Mr. Fox to a nearby table, she tried not to ogle the lithe way he moved, a man comfortable in his own skin, confident that the world had been designed for him. They sat and she opened the book to a short section on George Washington's childhood.

"The children might be interested to know that his father died when he was only eleven years old," she said, pointing to a paragraph. "He had to take on a man's work at a young age."

Mr. Fox leaned over the book, and Fiona caught a whiff of homemade lye soap, like her mother used to make. She resisted the urge to nudge closer.

"They would certainly like that," Mr. Fox said. He turned his face toward her, their noses only inches apart. His breath hitched and he jumped backward, leaving a wide gap between them. "I would also like to impress them with President Washington's sense of integrity. Have thee also a copy of the story of the cherry tree?"

Fiona blinked several times, collecting herself and trying to decide how best to reply. She hated to disappoint Mr. Fox—the cherry tree was such an endearing story—but she couldn't resist the pull of facts.

"We do have a copy of Mr. Weems's biography of President Washington, but I'm afraid the cherry tree tale is just that—a tale. Mr. Weems invented it for his book."

To her surprise, rather than being disappointed, Mr. Fox laughed. "That is terribly ironic," he said, his eyes dancing. Fiona laughed along with him.

"It certainly is."

Over the next quarter hour or so, Fiona and Mr. Fox chatted about George Washington and drew up a list of facts for him to share with the children. Fiona had once thought of becoming a teacher herself, and she enjoyed helping devise the lesson. And it certainly didn't hurt that Mr. Fox was such an engaging and handsome collaborator.

"I shall be eager to hear how the children enjoyed the lesson when you bring them by next week," she said as Mr. Fox gathered his notes to leave. She had barely begun to stack the books they'd been using when Nicole swooped over and snatched them up, immediately returning them to their proper places on the shelves. Fiona shook her head. She'd never be able to find another clerk as adept at the job as Nicole.

"I shall provide thee a full report," Mr. Fox said, shifting his notes under his arm. He glanced around, his gaze resting briefly on Nicole only a few feet away. His expression set in a look of determination like he'd just decided something, and he flicked his eyes back to Fiona, his face softening with that warm smile she'd noticed when he first walked in. "Forgive me if this is too forward, Fiona Ellicott, but might thee be free for a cup of coffee? There's a lovely café right 'round the corner." He inclined his head. "They also make a delicious drinking chocolate, if thee is more inclined that way."

Irritation prickled up Fiona's spine. She'd been so enjoying speaking with Mr. Fox, and then he had to do this. Why were all the men in this city under the impression that a woman with a job must be in desperate need of a suitor? If she had a penny for every time a male patron asked her out, she could single-handedly restore Mount Vernon. Just because she dared be visible in public and—gasp!—speak to men she didn't know, it didn't mean she was on the hunt for a husband. Especially when taking a husband would mean giving up her vocation, giving up *everything* she'd worked so hard for. She set her face into the stern expression she usually reserved for patrons whose conversations grew too loud.

"That is entirely too forward, Mr. Fox," she said, accentuating each syllable of his name like staccato notes. Her blood rose at the sound of her own voice. She might not have any power outside of this library, but within these walls, she was in charge, and she intended to wield that power. "This is a library, sir. A place of scholarship, and I am its head scholar. If you are looking for...*companionship*, I recommend you try Madam Hall's establishment on Maryland Avenue. I overhear many congressmen speaking favorably of the girls there."

Behind her, Fiona heard Nicole gasp, but she was too busy watching Mr. Fox's jaw working up and down to turn around.

"I assure thee, I wasn't attempting to...I..." He stared at her, a horrified expression on his face, and Fiona immediately regretted her sharp words. But it was too late to take them back. Mr. Fox stammered once more, then turned and strode out of the library, head down and shoulders hunched, at a pace just barely slow enough to be called a "walk."

She should run after him and apologize, beg forgiveness, offer to come to the orphanage and read stories to the children. But her feet were stuck in place as if she'd sunk ankle deep in the thick, sticky mud that often mired the streets of Washington.

Just before Mr. Fox disappeared through the towering doors of the West Wing, something white fluttered from his pocket and drifted to the floor.

Chapter Two

Caleb questioned himself the entire walk back to Georgetown.

Where had he erred? Fiona Ellicott had been so welcoming and helpful and seemed genuinely interested in the school. Even if she weren't interested in him personally, he thought she might at least enjoy an opportunity to speak at more length about the children.

Though he *had* been hoping she was interested in him personally.

Maybe he should have given her a warning of some kind before extending the invitation. But what sort of warning did a man give to a woman before asking her to coffee? He hadn't invited a woman anywhere in nearly ten years, not since Eliza Pennington's father had declared him too bookish to be of practical use and turned down Caleb's request to court the young lady. After that, Caleb had busied himself on his family's farm outside Philadelphia, trusting that the right woman would come along eventually.

She never had.

Finally, five years ago, at the behest of an elder at his Meeting, he'd come to Georgetown to help open the home. Here was an opportunity to put his bookishness to work for the good of society. The home and school kept him so busy—he was the first friendly adult face many of these poor children had ever seen—that he hadn't had time for courting. And apparently, he was now out of practice.

When he reached Foggy Bottom, he paused before crossing the bridge over Rock Creek into Georgetown. He'd been charging down the sidewalk since leaving the Castle, and he needed to catch his breath. He leaned against a building and pulled out his plain handkerchief to wipe the sweat that had accumulated on his brow despite the chill in the afternoon air. The white fabric was gray with dust from the library, so Caleb shoved it back in his pocket. He hated using the special one, but desperate times called for desperate measures, he supposed. And he could rinse out a little sweat once he got home. He reached into his other pocket for it, but his fingers found nothing but the pocket seam.

Icy dread coursed through him. He swept his fingers along the bottom of his pocket a second time but still didn't feel the familiar soft square of the embroidered handkerchief. He checked his other pocket again to no avail. Trying not to panic, he shook out the plain handkerchief, thinking perhaps the embroidered one was stuck to it, but no luck. Both of his coat pockets also turned up empty.

He must have dropped it somewhere along the way. He chewed on his lower lip. There was no choice but to retrace his steps, looking for it. Hopefully he'd dropped it on a sidewalk and it hadn't blown into the mucky street. A hard lump rose in his throat at the thought of Ruth's beautiful embroidery being trampled into the mud under a horse's hoofs.

Swallowing hard, he retraced his steps down Pennsylvania Avenue, his eyes darting between the sidewalk and the macadam street, which, thanks to all the rain they'd had lately, was inches deep in mud. His hopes soared when he spotted a white square on the sidewalk near the President's House, but they plummeted again when he saw it was just a handbill for a play. His blood rising, he crumpled it into a ball and flung it into the muddy street.

How could he have been so foolish as to lose the handkerchief? The one irreplaceable item he owned, and now it was gone. The corners of his eyes burned, blurring his vision, and he took several deep, gulping breaths. He still had a few blocks to cover. He might yet find the handkerchief.

He passed the President's House and turned right onto Twelfth Street, still scanning for any speck of white cotton. But as he crossed the bridge over the canal, holding his breath against the putrid stench, and covered the final blocks to the Smithsonian, the last of his hope dwindled. There was no sign of the handkerchief anywhere. He supposed it was possible he'd dropped it inside the Castle, but the building was now closed for the evening. He'd have to return in the morning and hope someone had turned it in to the desk in whichever department he'd dropped it in—which meant he'd likely have to ask at the library. He groaned. Maybe if he stopped by at lunchtime, he'd be lucky enough to avoid Fiona Ellicott and be able to speak with her assistant instead. As it was, he wasn't sure he'd survive the trip into the library with the children next week. He didn't believe he'd done anything wrong in asking the librarian to coffee, but he'd certainly embarrassed himself somehow.

Sighing, he turned back around and was startled to see lamplighters plying their trade, sending the falling darkness scuttling back from little halos of yellow light. He yanked his watch from his vest pocket, thinking how he should have also attached his handkerchief to his person by a small chain, and felt a jolt of panic when he read the time. Nearly 7:00 p.m. His journey back to the National Mall from Foggy Bottom had taken him almost an hour, and now he'd not only missed supper at the school, but everyone was likely to have started worrying about him. He rubbed his temples and, head down, started trudging back toward Georgetown.

He'd barely crossed the canal again when he heard someone shout his name from the street. He looked up and spotted a familiar, dark-haired figure driving a buggy. His friend Jacob Carter waved to him and beckoned him over.

"Let me drive you home," Jacob called.

A measure of relief washed through Caleb. At least he'd end today with a friendly face. He picked his way carefully through the mud to Jacob's buggy and climbed onto the seat next to his friend. His spirits lifted a tad as Jacob grinned at him and shook his hand.

"What brings thee out this way?" Caleb asked, suspecting he already knew the answer. A few years older than Caleb, Jacob was a physician who lived and worked in Georgetown, not far from the Friends' home. He typically didn't stray into Washington City, saying the health risks from the canal were simply too great.

"Looking for you," Jacob said, confirming Caleb's suspicion. "I was at the school today to check on Spryly. The children were worried when you weren't back for supper, so I offered to come look for you." He slapped the reins across his horse's back, and Caleb grabbed the edge of the seat as the buggy lurched forward.

"How is Spryly?" Caleb asked, hoping Jacob wouldn't press him for details about his day. He'd have to answer truthfully, and he'd rather not relive it. And he was genuinely concerned about the little cricket. He knew he shouldn't have favorites among the children, but the seven-year-old was a charmer.

"Still coughing," Jacob said. "But at least he's not worsening. I left a bottle of whiskey with Regina for you to dose him with, and I'll come by tomorrow to check on him again."

Caleb tried to hold back a frown, but Jacob had a keen eye for changes in facial expressions—probably from years of searching for clues to patients' ailments—and he chuckled.

"I know, but *you* know I wouldn't ask you to handle liquor if it weren't absolutely necessary. It'll help the poor little fellow sleep, and a couple nights of good sleep will go a long way toward helping him shake off this bronchitis."

Caleb knew Jacob was right. The physician had prescribed the same remedy for Spryly this time last year. Seemed as though the boy came down with bronchitis every year when the weather started to turn chilly. The best thing for him would be to get out of this filthy city and the horrible miasma that wafted up from the canal. The orphanage was three miles away, but they could still smell it if the wind was blowing the right direction. But unless a family wandered in from the country looking to adopt a sickly boy, there seemed little hope that Spryly would make it out of the city any time soon. He'd already been at the home for four years since Jacob had found him roaming Pennsylvania Avenue near the President's House on one of his rare trips into the city. Based on the toddler's grimy, emaciated state, it was obvious he'd been abandoned, and Jacob had immediately bundled him off to the Friends' home, where Spryly had lived ever since.

"I will be sure to give him the dosage," Caleb said.

"Good man." Jacob nodded once. Out of his peripheral vision, Caleb saw Jacob flick his eyes toward him. He stifled a groan, sensing the question before Jacob asked it. "What held you up? Regina said she expected you back well before supper."

Caleb pinched the bridge of his nose. "I dropped my handkerchief somewhere—either in the Castle or on the way to Foggy Bottom—and I was looking for it."

Jacob snapped his head around to look at Caleb full on, his face full of concern. "Did you find it?"

Caleb's throat felt suddenly tight, and all he could do was shake his head.

"Oh, Caleb, I'm so sorry." Jacob took both reins in one hand and squeezed Caleb's shoulder with the other. "I know how much it meant to you."

Caleb nodded and swallowed hard. "It was all that remained of her. The only evidence of a life lived."

"A beautiful life," Jacob said. Caleb heard him swallow too. Ruth had been special to everyone who knew her, and no one had fought harder to save her than Jacob.

They fell into silence for the next half mile or so. Jacob was so good at holding silence that Caleb thought it a shame he was a Methodist. The doctor would make an excellent Quaker.

As they drove out of Foggy Bottom and across Rock Creek, Jacob chatted about a book he'd recently finished. Caleb only caught about every third word his friend said.

He knew that rumination would do nothing to put Ruth's embroidered handkerchief back in his pocket, but he couldn't help but dwell on it and the memories of that sweet girl. Jacob must have sensed his sadness because he reached over and squeezed Caleb's shoulder a second time and didn't speak again until they reached the orphanage.

A small flock of children fluttered out through the front doors of the home when Jacob and Caleb drove into the yard. Martha, a dark-haired girl of thirteen, led the pack, with Jacob's fourteen-year-old daughter, Lyddie, bringing up the rear, a book clutched in her hand. The flock encircled Caleb as soon as he jumped down from the buggy.

"Where were you?" Martha asked.

"We were so worried!" a red-haired boy added.

Caleb assured the children he was fine, he'd merely gotten held up, and looked up in time to see Regina Hogarth, the home's head cook and unofficial mother, striding toward him.

"Where was thee?" she said, her face etched with concern. "I was beginning to worry thee had fallen into that horrid canal."

"I do expect it to swallow us all someday," Jacob said from behind him.

Caleb repeated his line about getting held up. Regina deserved a more thorough explanation, but he didn't wish to recount the entire story here in front of the children, most of whom had also known and loved Ruth. He could tell her later as the children prepared for bed.

"Spryly's been asking for you, Caleb," Lyddie said. "I didn't tell him you were overdue, but I think he sensed something was amiss. I promised him I'd send you up as soon as you were available."

Caleb smiled for the first time since he'd lost his handkerchief. Jacob's daughter was a remarkable young lady, often accompanying her father on his rounds to the home so she could read to the younger children. Caleb suspected she might follow in her father's footsteps and become a doctor. Several medical colleges accepted women now, and Caleb hoped they might soon be allowed to vote as well. It was past time the world recognized the value of women.

"I'll head right up," he said.

"What about thy supper?" Regina asked, though it was more of an order than a question. Despite being a short woman so slight she was at risk of being swept away by a strong breeze, Regina Hogarth was a force to be reckoned with. Especially when she wore the stern expression now on her countenance.

"I will be quick," Caleb said and held up the whiskey bottle. "Once I set the boy's mind at ease and give him his medicine, I shall eat a hearty meal." He regretted the words as soon as they escaped his lips. He didn't feel like eating a single bite, yet he'd just committed himself to finishing a large serving of whatever Regina had cooked up. At least she was an excellent cook and a marvel at making delicious meals out of the humble ingredients the Friends' home could provide.

He thanked Jacob for carting him home and bid the doctor and Lyddie goodbye, glad that they lived only a few blocks away. They'd be late getting home because of him even without a long drive. He shook his head. It was unlike him to be so melancholy. The weight of the day must be catching up to him.

He and Regina herded the children back inside, and Regina ordered them all to wash up for bed. Caleb mounted the stairs to the home's small infirmary to check on Spryly. The little imp's color did look better, but he broke into a coughing fit as he shouted hello. Caleb quickly poured a shot of whiskey and coaxed the boy into swallowing it. With only a bit of mild cursing—the children who came in off the streets always knew the most unique language—the little boy downed the whiskey and nuzzled back against his pillows.

"Gotta be careful runnin' off like that," Spryly said, the tone of his voice wise beyond his years. "One day you'll get so lost you won't never be able to find your way home."

Caleb tilted his head. "Is that what happened to thee?" Like too many of the children, Spryly's origins were a mystery, and Caleb always hoped he might remember something that would at least give him a sense of where he came from. Better still if the memory included a loving parent.

Spryly coughed and shrugged his thin shoulders. "Dunno. But it's as good an explanation as any, don't you figure?"

Caleb chuckled. The child never failed to cheer him up. He was like a character straight out of a Dickens novel, which is probably why when at three years old, the boy had declared his name to be "Spryly Wriggler," no one at the home had challenged him. Caleb tousled Spryly's curly brown hair and told him to sleep well.

"I expect you'll feel a good bit better in the morning," he said.

Spryly fixed him with a stare that Caleb swore bore straight into his soul. "Caleb? I bet you will too."

Chapter Three

There had been no avoiding Nicole's glower. After Mr. Fox hightailed it out of the library yesterday, Fiona's colleague had fixed her with a glare so icy it could have frozen the sludge in the canal.

"You need to apologize to that man," Nicole had said, her sharp whisper somehow more piercing than if she had shouted for the entire library to hear. "Turning down his offer of coffee was your prerogative, but he did nothing to warrant the insinuations you made."

Fiona's already red cheeks warmed further. If Nicole's stare could freeze the canal, her own face could thaw it again. The worst part was that Nicole was right. She certainly had every right to turn Mr. Fox down for coffee, but she hadn't needed to snap at him. It wasn't his fault Nicole was leaving, and he'd even mentioned the need for women's equality and been impressed by her position at the Smithsonian. She stifled a groan. She'd have to hire a cab and go to the Friends' home to apologize and return the man's handkerchief. She'd picked it up after he fled and recognized the bright embroidery from when he'd pulled it out of his pocket while they were looking at books. She tried to catch him, but a senator's clerk stopped her with an urgent question. By the time she passed him off to Nicole and made it outside, Mr. Fox was long gone.

She'd stood outside in the watery sunlight filtering

through the gray sky and studied the handkerchief. The monogram was expertly stitched—a sign that whoever had made it for him had taken great care. But why would a man—a *Quaker* of all people, who were known for their honesty—ask a woman to coffee when he already had someone special? No good reason that Fiona could think of. Though maybe his mother had made it.

In any event, it was none of her affair. Her obligation extended only to returning the handkerchief and delivering her apology. Then she could return to the Castle and her work as if nothing had ever happened. She could find some reason to be in another department on Wednesday when Mr. Fox brought the children to see the library. Nicole could show them around. Fiona need never see Mr. Fox again.

Strangely, her heart had sunk at the thought.

Now, as she and Nicole bustled around, preparing the library to close for the day, a burst of butterflies twittered around Fiona's stomach. She planned to head out to Georgetown immediately after work today, hoping to catch Mr. Fox at the orphanage before the hour grew too late. The butterflies fluttered faster as she climbed into a cab and faster still as the cab crossed the creek into Georgetown. She found herself frequently reaching into her skirt pocket and stroking the soft cotton of the handkerchief, her fingertips occasionally running over the bumps of the embroidery. Mr. Fox's mother must have made it for him. He certainly wouldn't have invited her to coffee if he had a sweetheart—or worse, a wife.

She shook her head. Mr. Fox's romantic situation didn't concern her, no matter how handsome he was.

She shook her head again. She must be overtired.

The cab pulled up to the Friends' home just before

six o'clock, and Fiona spotted a couple children playing on the small lawn in front of the red-brick three-story building, hardly bigger than most homes in Georgetown. A little shot of surprise coursed through her. Given the number of parentless children in the city, she'd expected the orphanage to be much larger. But then again, the home had been open only a few years. No one knew better than a government employee how long it could take to get the space one truly needed for their endeavors.

A chorus of children's voices raised in song drifted toward her, and she looked to one side and spotted a small cluster of children in a corner of the yard under a large oak tree. Directing them was a girl no older than twelve or thirteen, a plait of dark hair trailing down her back nearly to her waist. Fiona wandered toward them, enchanted by the children's perfect harmony as the girl led them in "Molly, Do You Love Me."

She'd never expected music. Not here at an orphanage, a place one would expect to be devoid of joy. And especially not so close to Washington City, whose fug often wafted into Georgetown—a fug that had been both literal and metaphorical since John Brown's attack. Washington City had never been a particularly pleasant city to live in, but the morale of the townspeople seemed to have reached a new low over the concerns of a possible war.

But here, at an orphanage run by people who typically eschewed music, was hope and joy in the form of song. Fiona felt her heart lift, and she couldn't tear her eyes away from the little group until they'd finished their piece. When the dark-haired girl lowered her arms from her conductor's pose, Fiona burst into applause. The boys and girls facing her broke into grins, and the dark-haired girl turned and met Fiona's gaze. The girl's eyes were nearly as dark as her hair, and a sprinkle of freckles dusted her nose. Fiona gasped. She could have been looking at herself at the same age.

"Good evening, ma'am," the girl said, smiling. "May I help you?"

Fiona blinked as if coming out of a trance. "I apologize. I did not mean to interrupt. Please, continue your singing."

The girl's nose wrinkled as her smile broadened. "It's quite all right. We were just finishing. It's nearly time for supper." She turned to the group of younger children and waved them toward the house with instructions to wash up. The children flitted away like a flock of sparrows, many of them casting glances over their shoulders at Fiona. "Are you looking for someone, ma'am?"

"Yes," Fiona said. "Mr. Caleb Fox. I have something of his I need to return." No need to tell the young lady that she also needed to apologize for poor behavior. She'd be humiliating herself enough in just a few moments.

The girl's eyes brightened. "Of course! Please come. I'll take you inside and fetch him for you." She beckoned to Fiona, who fell into step next to her as they headed toward the house. "I'm Martha Dawson, by the way. May I ask your name so I might tell Caleb who's calling?"

Martha's use of the director's Christian name rather than "Mr. Fox" caught Fiona off guard. She'd never heard a child address an adult so familiarly. Her surprise must have registered on her face because Martha laughed.

"It sounds strange to everyone at first," she said. "But as Quakers believe we are all equal in the eyes of God, they don't use titles with one another." She shrugged. "None of us children are Friends, but we've fallen in line with most of their customs. Except for not singing. I don't think I could live without music." She sighed and waved her hands in front of her, fingers fluttering as if across the keys of a piano.

They climbed the wooden steps onto a small porch and stepped through the front door into a dim hallway. Laughter echoed from somewhere upstairs, and the tantalizing, unmistakable scent of simmering beef and potatoes wafted past Fiona's nose. Her mouth watered. She hoped her older sister, Susan, was cooking up something delicious right now for when she returned home.

Martha led her into a small parlor and gestured to an armchair with faded green upholstery. "If you'd like to sit down, I'll go find Caleb. Your name, though, ma'am?"

Fiona sat gingerly as the chair squeaked underneath her. "Miss Fiona Ellicott," she said. "Of the Smithsonian Library." She wasn't certain why she felt the need to add the last part. Mr. Fox was unlikely to forget her name any time soon.

Martha's face lit up. "The Smithsonian Library? You work there?"

Fiona nodded and Martha's smile split into a wide grin. "Oh, you must tell me all about it. Have you a lot of books? Well, I suppose you must, it's the *Smithsonian*. What's your favorite book? Have you ever met an author? Do the authors come to visit their books? Do you get to read them all before the patrons do?"

Fiona's laughter interrupted the girl's rapid questioning. The child was like her in more than just appearance. Martha ducked her head.

"My apologies, Miss Ellicott. I'll fetch Caleb for you."

Fiona reached out and grasped Martha's wrist before the girl could stride away. "I shall be happy to show you the library sometime and answer all your questions." She nearly mentioned the planned trip next week, but after what happened between herself and Mr. Fox yesterday, she wasn't certain he still planned to bring the children to the Castle. But surely he'd agree to let her take Martha there for an afternoon.

Martha's grin returned, and when Fiona released her wrist, she scampered away.

Waiting those last few moments before delivering an apology always felt like an eternity, and Fiona sat in the parlor for at least two centuries before she heard footsteps coming down the stairs. Another decade and a half passed before Mr. Fox's form filled the narrow doorway.

Gracious, she'd forgotten how green his eyes were. Even from a distance of a few feet, she could see them shimmering in the dim lamplight. His jaw was dusted with evening whiskers and his shoulders drooped as though with fatigue. He snapped straight when their eyes met.

"Miss Ellicott," he said, striding forward, right hand extended. She accepted it and allowed him to help her to her feet, ignoring the tingle that shot up her arm at his touch. "How may I be of service?"

Her spine went ramrod straight. He'd used a title, calling her "Miss Ellicott" instead of "Fiona Ellicott" like he had yesterday at the library. Goodness, she must have scared him terribly. Either that or he was deliberately keeping her at a distance. Regardless, she found herself longing to hear her first name on his lips. But no time for that now, she reminded herself. She mustn't lose sight of her mission here. She steeled herself with a deep breath.

"It is I who owe you a service, Mr. Fox," she said, sliding her hand reluctantly from his grasp. "I must apologize. While I certainly had the right to decline, I should not have spoken to you as I did yesterday. Your offer was kind and, I believe, innocently intended, and I should have treated it as such. I am sorry."

He stared at her as if she'd suddenly sprouted a beard, and she realized that he must have thought she'd come to verbally thrash him again. A pang of guilt pulsed deep in her chest, but it melted away when Mr. Fox broke into a wide, brilliant smile.

"I thank thee, and I wish to offer an apology of my own. I clearly startled thee yesterday, and that was never my intention."

Fiona broke into a smile, too, relieved that he didn't seem to harbor any ill feelings. And she'd never known a man to apologize willingly to a woman before, not for rejecting his advances, anyway. An interesting man, this Caleb Fox.

"I appreciate thee came all this way to speak with me in person," he said, "when a telegram certainly would have sufficed."

"I'm afraid it wouldn't have. You dropped something on your way out yesterday, and I needed to return it." She dipped her hand into her pocket, withdrew the embroidered handkerchief, and held it out to him. He gasped and reached for it with trembling fingers. He plucked it from her grasp and unfolded it, running a finger reverently over the bright stitching.

"It was in the library after all," he whispered. When he looked up at Fiona, tears glistened in the corners of his eyes. "I searched the streets for over an hour. I thought never to see it again." He swallowed. "I cannot thank thee enough."

Fiona shifted her weight, taken aback by Mr. Fox's display of emotion. She'd guessed the handkerchief was special, but she'd clearly underestimated how much.

"You're quite welcome," she said. "I suspected it held sentimental value, so it was only right I return it."

Mr. Fox nodded, folded the handkerchief gently, and tucked it into his pocket. "I thank thee," he said again. He stared at the floor for a moment, then cleared his throat and looked up, the traces of the tears gone from his eyes. "Where are my manners? Thee has come all this way to do me a great favor. Please, join us for supper."

Fiona desperately wanted to accept. She'd love to meet more of the children. Were they all as curious as Martha? Even if they weren't, Fiona was certain she could find plenty at the library to interest them. She spent so much of her days digging up obscure records and volumes for stuffy scholars that she'd love to spend a day or two finding books to delight the children. Much like she'd done with Mr. Fox yesterday, she realized.

She never should have turned him down for coffee.

Her mouth dropped open at the thought. What was she thinking? She was committed to her work, and as a woman, she had to choose between work and romance. She did not have a man's luxury to choose both.

"I wish I could," she said, "but my family will worry

if I'm not home soon." This was true. Susan, her brother-in-law, and her two nieces would fret if she were much later than she was already going to be. The streets of Washington weren't safe after dark—there were too many rioters, petty thieves, and firehouse gangs for the miniscule police force to keep in check. A woman moving through the city alone at night could find herself in trouble.

Mr. Fox's eyes lost a touch of their sparkle. "Of course. We certainly wouldn't want to cause them concern."

The disappointment in his face was like a stab to the heart, and Fiona knew that even though she could never indulge herself in sentimental feelings toward Mr. Fox, she wanted to know more about this man who had devoted his life to caring for orphaned children. Remarkable children at that, if the unexpected concert in the yard was any indication.

"Perhaps we could speak further on Wednesday when you bring the children to the Smithsonian? I'd like to hear how they enjoyed their lesson on George Washington."

A glimmer returned to Mr. Fox's eyes and his brows lifted. "I would enjoy that very much."

Fiona smiled, delighted that she could make him happy. "Then I shall look forward to seeing you on Wednesday, Mr. Fox."

"On one condition," he said, one corner of his mouth quirking up in a playful smile.

"What's that?"

"Thee must call me Caleb."

Chapter Four

Caleb's stomach whirled with nerves as he led his gaggle of children toward the Smithsonian Library on Fourth Day afternoon. They'd already toured the museum in the main lobby, where the children enjoyed the taxidermied birds along with the minerals and shells and, to Spryly's great delight, a few mummies.

Spryly was still coughing more than Caleb would like, but Jacob said he could come along on this outing so long as he wore a warm jacket and rode in a carriage to the Smithsonian and back. Caleb rarely parted with money for cabs—he had two perfectly good feet, after all—but he couldn't bear to leave Spryly behind, so he sent the boy ahead in a cab with Martha while the rest of them walked the three miles or so to the Institution.

Spryly kept up a steady stream of cough-punctuated questions about the exhibits all morning—especially in the apparatus room on the second floor—prompting Caleb to seek out an employee more than once. The day was warm, probably the last mild day they'd have until spring, and they'd savored a picnic lunch on the Castle's lawn.

Caleb still couldn't believe that Fiona, as she'd said he could call her, had reunited him with his handkerchief. He'd truly thought it gone forever. Despite his embarrassment, he'd planned to return to the library the day after he dropped it last week, but two other children besides Spryly started feeling poorly—there seemed to be an early-season cold going around—and Regina couldn't tend them and substitute teach for him at the same time. He'd been devastated, moping around all day, unable to get excited even over the new art supplies a member of the Meeting had donated for the children.

And then Fiona arrived with Ruth's handkerchief in perfect condition and restored a little piece of his soul.

He slipped his hand into his pocket frequently today, checking that the handkerchief was still safe and sound. He didn't intend to ever lose it again.

As they made their way into the West Wing, Caleb also intended to have that chat with Fiona about the lesson on George Washington. He would have been embarrassed to admit to anyone how badly he wanted to speak with her some more. Even if he had to do it with a dozen children orbiting him and, at least in Spryly's case, memorizing everything he and Fiona said to each other.

Fiona met them in the massive doorway leading into the library. She was resplendent in a light-gray dress patterned with pink and yellow flowers. Two tendrils of dark hair had escaped her loose bun and framed her long, oval face. When she smiled and said, "Good afternoon," Caleb felt his mouth stretch into a wide grin. He squared his shoulders and strode to Fiona, extending his hand.

"Good afternoon, Fiona Ellicott." He shook her hand, trying to ignore how soft and warm her palm was. "Lovely to see thee again." Behind him, he was certain he heard Martha giggle. "May I introduce the children? I believe thee has met Martha."

"So happy to see you again," Fiona said, smiling at the girl.

Caleb introduced the children one by one, except for Spryly, who stepped forward and introduced himself.

"Spryly Wriggler," he announced, shaking Fiona's hand with the vigor of a politician up for reelection. "Pleasure to meet you." His skinny chest hopped, and Caleb could tell he was trying to hold back a cough. He frowned. Maybe he should have left Spryly at home after all.

But then Fiona glanced over Spryly's head and caught Caleb's eye. The corners of her mouth twitched, and Caleb knew she was holding back a laugh—such was a common reaction to meeting Spryly—and he was glad he'd let the boy come along. The outing was good for him *and* Fiona, it would seem.

"I gotta say, though, Miss, that I'm a mite disappointed by your castle here," Spryly said.

Fiona lifted her brows, and Caleb could tell she was still fighting to keep from laughing. "I'm deeply sorry to hear that, Mr. Wriggler. Might I inquire as to the nature of your disappointment?"

Spryly fixed a gaze on her that clearly expressed disbelief that he had to explain. "Don't got a moat."

Caleb snorted and tried, unsuccessfully, judging by the glare Martha leveled on him, to disguise it as a sneeze. Spryly had been so excited to see, as he called it, a "gen-u-wine" castle that Caleb had been wondering why the boy looked so disgruntled when they arrived. Now he knew.

"Mr. Wriggler," Fiona said, her voice serious, "I couldn't agree with you more, and I intend to take your concern straight to Secretary Clark himself at my earliest opportunity. In the meantime, if it's moats you're interested in, might I show you some diagrams of castles in Europe? We've a book in our collection that has several."

Spryly grinned, exposing the large gap in the front of his mouth where he was waiting for a tooth to come in. "Miss Ellicott, ma'am, I'd be delighted." He crooked his left arm and offered it to Fiona, who, with a smile at Caleb, took it and allowed Spryly to escort her into the library. As they crossed the threshold, Spryly glanced over his shoulder and smiled smugly.

Caleb bit down hard on his lower lip to hold in a bark of laughter. The little imp! He was going to have to keep a close eye on Spryly when the boy got a bit older. Then Spryly coughed again, and Caleb grimaced, silently praying that Spryly would grow old enough for him to have to keep close watch on his comings and goings.

He ushered the rest of the children into the library behind Spryly and Fiona and grinned when he heard their astonished gasps as they took in the soaring ceiling with its series of skylights, the tall, arched windows running the lengths of the rich, red walls, and, of course, the hundreds and hundreds of books. The shelves were arranged in two-story alcoves, and Caleb appreciated the efficient use of the vertical space in the room.

Still on Spryly's arm, Fiona led the group to a shelf about halfway down the length of the room and pulled a key ring from her dress pocket. Without even glancing at the keys themselves, she selected one and inserted it into the lock on the shelf's glass door.

"Ma'am," a ten-year-old boy named Eric asked, "why are the books locked up?"

Fiona turned to him, a little frown on her face. "Unfortunately, we've experienced what Secretary Clark calls 'a lamentable want of honesty.' The books used to be freely available to anyone who wandered in off the street, but patrons were tearing out pages to save copying information by hand, and some books were stolen altogether. We'll never be able to expand our collection if we spend all our funding on replacements, so we had to lock them up."

"That's terribly dishonest," Eric said, making Caleb smile.

"And shows a blatant disregard for the future needs of others," Martha added, broadening Caleb's smile. The children weren't required to join the Religious Society of Friends, but Caleb was pleased that some of the Quaker values were rubbing off anyway.

Fiona unlocked the case and withdrew a book that she handed to Spryly. "Here you are, young man. Castles with moats. Enjoy." She smiled and pointed him toward a nearby table. Eric and a couple other boys followed him, and they were soon crowded around the book, exclaiming over the illustrations.

One by one, Fiona found books for each of the children, either individually or in small groups, until only Martha remained by Caleb's side.

"How about you, Martha?" Fiona said. "What does your mind cry out for?"

Martha gazed at her, eyes wide with admiration. She chewed her lower lip for a moment as if she were afraid to ask. "Mozart," she said at last, her voice breathy. "Have you got any books about Mozart?"

Fiona broke into a wide smile. "My dear," she said, extending her hand, "I have *six*."

Martha gasped and grabbed Fiona's hand. Caleb's heart swelled as he watched his young charge fairly skip alongside the librarian while they made their way to another bank of shelves farther down the long room. Next to him, Spryly and Eric debated the merits of different castle constructions, and two tables down, little Patricia hummed to herself and twirled a finger in her hair while leafing through a copy of *Grimm's Fairy Tales*. He took it all in, these orphaned children with tragic pasts and uncertain futures, their burdens and worries lifted for at least a few moments.

The library was a magical place.

He would never be able to thank Fiona enough for this visit, but he certainly hoped she'd let him try.

Nearly at the opposite end of the long room, Martha let out a squeal that echoed through the entire West Wing. Caleb felt his eyebrows shoot up. Martha wasn't given to outbursts, and at thirteen, she was certainly old enough to know better even if she were. He hustled over, intending to remind her to be mindful of the other patrons in the library. When he reached her, though, she and Fiona were giggling together.

"Sorry," Martha stage-whispered to Caleb. "It's just that Miss Ellicott said they have a *piano* here." Her eyes shone with such joy that Caleb immediately forgot his irritation.

"Have they?" he said, his smile returning.

Martha nodded so vigorously Caleb marveled that she didn't sprain her neck.

"We were discussing Mozart, and Martha mentioned that she knew how to play the piano," Fiona said. "She was quite excited when I told her we have a Steinway in the lecture room upstairs."

Caleb felt his eyebrows lift again. Martha's parents had been musicians, dying together one night in a fire at a music hall where they were performing. Martha was only ten at the time, but from what she said, she'd already become competent on the piano. Unfortunately, the Friends rarely used music in their worship, so the home had no way for Martha to continue her studies. She'd taken it upon herself to teach the other children to sing, often in beautiful harmony, but Caleb knew she missed playing the piano. He caught Fiona's eye, hoping for Martha's sake that she was about to make the offer he felt pulsing in the air between them.

"Martha," Fiona said, not breaking from Caleb's gaze, "why don't you take this book to that table over there and look at it? I need to speak with Mr. Fox for a moment."

Chapter Five

Fiona suspected Secretary Clark would be amenable to her plan, but just in case, she hadn't made Caleb any promises. In truth, she hadn't told Caleb much of anything at all, only that she had an idea involving the children and would he like to meet for that coffee soon?

The man's jaw had dropped so low that for a moment Fiona thought she might have to help him pick it up off the floor. But after the way she'd turned him down last week, she supposed it was only natural for him to be shocked.

His green eyes had lit up brilliantly as they nearly popped out of his head, and a lock of his combed-back dark hair had come loose and drooped over his forehead, almost into his eyes. She smiled, remembering the way he'd hastily shoved it back into place. She'd nearly forgotten herself and her professional position and called him "Caleb" instead of "Mr. Fox." She'd agreed last week to call him by his first name, but it didn't seem proper when he was patronizing the library.

She could hardly believe she'd agreed to call him "Caleb" at all, let alone allow him to call her "Fiona." Her older sister would have been scandalized had she known how familiar Fiona had become with a man she barely knew. But Caleb was so sincere, so genuine, that calling him "Mr. Fox" felt more pretentious than proper. And she liked the thought of being familiar with him, even if they could never be more than colleagues.

And she hoped they would be, at least temporarily… If she could talk Secretary Clark into going along with her idea.

After closing up the library on Friday afternoon, two days after the children's visit, she headed for the East Wing of the Castle. Out of habit, she took shallower breaths as she approached the Laboratory of Natural History, and, also out of habit, thanked her lucky stars that the library was on the opposite end of the building from the malodorous lab.

She'd wanted to speak with the secretary the moment Caleb and the children departed the library, but Secretary Clark was so busy during the week. Receiving visiting scientists, overseeing the ever-evolving exhibits, and chairing various committees kept him flitting from one area of the Castle to another. Fiona knew she would have a much better chance of holding his full attention if she waited until the end of the week to speak with him. And Caleb wouldn't be able to meet her at the café until next Thursday anyway, so there really was no rush.

Just as she'd hoped, she spotted Secretary Clark heading for the private staircase that led to his family's apartment on the second floor. She called his name.

"Might I have a quick word?"

The secretary turned and broke into his familiar, warm smile.

"Miss Ellicott," he said, walking toward her. He tucked the newspaper he was carrying under his arm and clasped her outstretched hand in both of his. Even at sixty-two years old, Alexander Clark carried himself with the posture and stride of a much younger man who expected he might discover something life-changing just around the next corner—as well he might. Secretary Clark was a celebrated chemist himself, and he worked tirelessly to support young scientists in their research, often finding places for them to live in the Castle while they conducted their experiments. Sadly, he had no time to conduct his own research, but Fiona had no doubt that countless future inventions would owe their discovery to this man and his tireless advocacy for American science.

"How may I assist you?" he asked now, his dark eyes twinkling under his thick, gray eyebrows. His hair, too, was a dark gray, but still as full as Fiona imagined it had been in his youth. With his straight nose, strong, cleft chin, and gentle sense of humor, she could understand what had attracted Mrs. Clark. She smiled back.

"Well sir, I'm not sure if you're aware, but a group of children from the Friends' Home School in Georgetown visited the Institution on Wednesday."

Secretary Clark's eyebrows lifted. "The orphanage?"

Fiona nodded. "Yes sir."

The corners of the secretary's mouth twitched downward in a small frown. "A shame I didn't know. I would have greeted them personally."

Fiona silently chastised herself for not informing her boss of the children's visit. Secretary Clark loved children—he had four of his own—and he certainly would have given them a warm welcome, likely making himself late for his appointments that day by insisting on showing them around the Castle himself.

"My apologies, sir, I'm ashamed to admit it hadn't crossed my mind. But," she continued, excitement thrumming through her, "I'm hoping to have them back."

Secretary Clark tilted his head, indicating to Fiona

that she had his full attention. She couldn't hold in the smile that stretched across her face.

"The children can sing, sir. Beautifully. I heard them when I visited the orphanage last week. And one of them, a young lady named Martha, knows how to play the piano." She took a deep breath, silently praying that this idea would sound as enticing when she said it aloud as it did in her mind. "I'd like to invite them to perform a Christmas concert here at the Castle. I've checked the schedule, and the lecture room is not engaged on December twenty-fourth. How lovely would it be to have the children perform on Christmas Eve?"

Secretary Clark's expression could have outshone the noonday sun. "Miss Ellicott, that is a wonderful idea! And so well timed. Look at this." He swept the newspaper from under his arm, unfolded it, and handed it to her. As she took it, he tapped a headline. "Trial of John Brown," he read aloud. "Dratted circus is sixty-five miles away, but you'd think it was being held on the Mall, to hear the newspapers tell it. Mrs. Clark and the girls have been wondering if they oughtn't leave the city in case of trouble, which there might be, no matter which way this goes. Either the slaveholders or the abolitionists will be upset by the verdict, and either side could erupt in violence—again—at any time."

Fiona's excitement over the concert faded in light of the secretary's words. He was right. Congress had been on edge for years already. Only a few years ago, poor Senator Charles Sumner had been beaten nearly to death by a representative from South Carolina who had taken umbrage at the senator's harsh words regarding slaveholders. Just last year, a horrible fight broke out on the floor of the House of Representatives, again over slavery. Now, with John Brown's attempted attack on slaveholders in Virginia, the whole city was jumpy. Brown's trial started yesterday, and it wasn't helping matters, even though it was being held in Virginia, not Washington.

"I agree with you, sir," Fiona said, returning the newspaper, "but I'm afraid I don't see how this relates to the children giving a Christmas concert."

The secretary's smile returned as he folded the paper and tucked it back under his arm. "I mean, Miss Ellicott, that this city could use a little joy. And I can think of nothing more joyful than children's voices raised in song to celebrate such a sacred time of year."

Fiona opened her mouth to thank him, but the secretary continued.

"And perhaps we could offer free admission and encourage patrons to instead leave donations or small gifts for the home. Give those poor children a nice Christmas."

Fiona had to fight to hold back a most unprofessional squeal of joy. Gracious, what was the matter with her? She'd never been prone to squealing, even as a girl. But no matter. The children were going to perform at the Smithsonian Institution on Christmas Eve. She couldn't wait to tell Caleb.

"Thank you, sir," she said, trying not to sound overly gushing. "Thank you so much."

Secretary Clark inclined his head, indicating that she was welcome. "I'll leave the preparations in your capable hands, Miss Ellicott. Please let me know if you or the children require anything."

Fiona thanked him again and was about to take her leave when she remembered her promise to Spryly.

"Actually, sir, there is one more thing."

The secretary lifted his eyebrows.

"One of the boys would like us to build a moat."

Alexander Clark threw back his head and laughed, the joyful sound echoing down the long hall. "He and I both, Miss Ellicott," he said. "He and I both."

****

Fiona spotted Caleb as soon as she entered the café the following afternoon. He sat at a small table near the front window, reading a newspaper and drumming his fingers on the dark wooden tabletop. A handful of other men—most likely congressional aides and clerks, this close to the Capitol—were scattered around the little shop's other tables. Most of them were trussed up with a peacock's array of colorful vests and cravats, and several shot a few derisive chuckles in Caleb's direction.

But if Caleb noticed them identifying him as an oddity, he clearly didn't care because when his eyes flicked up from his newspaper, his gaze went nowhere else but directly to hers. He leapt to his feet, his chair scraping loudly along the wooden floor, and he held her gaze for a moment before striding toward her, hands outstretched.

"Lovely to see thee again," he said, clasping her extended hand in his. The day was chilly, and Fiona relished the warmth of his hands through her gloves. "Please come and sit."

He led her to his table, and she appreciated that he'd chosen a spot in plain view rather than in a dark corner where it might look like they were having an assignation. She certainly didn't need one of these congressional aides recognizing her from the Institution—they often came to conduct research—and whispering around town that the Smithsonian's head librarian was having a covert affair. Such a scandal wouldn't harm a man in her position—or an even higher position, for that matter, given the number of senators chasing tail around Washington—but for her, it could spell disaster. Quite thoughtful of Caleb to consider that.

Though now that she watched him fold his newspaper, she realized he'd probably sat by the window simply because it had the best light for reading.

As a librarian, though, she could appreciate that too.

Caleb assisted her with her chair, then settled himself in the seat opposite her.

"I arrived early so I could catch up on the news," he said. As he rolled up the paper, Fiona caught a glimpse of one of the headlines: *John Brown's trial continues in Virginia*. She sighed.

"Is thee well?" Caleb asked, concern brimming in his eyes.

"Quite," Fiona said, cringing internally. She didn't want to spoil what should be a lovely meeting with a discussion of the recent…upheaval? Incident? Tragedy? She wasn't even sure what to call it. What was the term for the situation in which the country had so deliberately placed itself? Did such a term even exist? Caleb's reassuring voice interrupted her thoughts.

"The children say I'm a good listener."

She met his gaze and smiled. Something about his expression, his entire *presence*, was so open and sincere—so unusual in this city where everyone seemed to be interested only in what they could extort from others. He left her in absolute awe. And she found she couldn't muster an ounce of reluctance to divulge what was on her mind.

"It's this John Brown affair." She gestured toward the newspaper Caleb was now tucking into his coat pocket. "Such a nasty business." She chewed on her lower lip, trying to summon the words to describe her conflicted emotions. "I hate slavery. I hate how it debases human beings, and I fully support Mr. Brown's stance against it. But his tactics… Attacking the federal arsenal? Deliberately trying to spark a war?" She sighed again. "I understand his anger, but I fear his actions have only worsened the situation. This issue has been a powder keg for this nation since its inception, and I worry that he's lit a fuse."

Caleb's eyebrows lifted. "So, thee agrees with his stance but opposes his use of violence?"

"Precisely. Because it can't possibly improve the situation. If anything, slaveholders will re-commit themselves even more virulently to their position. Worse, I fear they may take it out on the very people Mr. Brown claimed to be trying to aid."

She was too young to remember Nat Turner's insurrection in Virginia in 1831, but she knew from her reading that after the uprising, slaveholders had cracked down hard on their slaves, passing laws prohibiting Negro literacy, disallowing them to travel, increasing violence against them to instill fear. Would John Brown's attempt to save them instead cause them further harm?

"I share thy concern," Caleb said. "Violence begets violence."

"It does," Fiona said. "The Southern states have threatened secession since…well, off and on throughout my entire life. I pray that the nation holds together, but if it cannot, then I pray the split is peaceful."

Surprisingly, Caleb smiled at this and reached across the table to take her hand in his. It was a strong, reassuring hand, and she found herself curling her fingers around it and holding on.

"As do I," he said, his voice softer now. "In the meantime, we must be the light."

Fiona let herself relax into his tender gaze. Who *was* this man? And why in the world was he in Washington City and not someplace gentler?

"May I get you something?" a male voice asked.

Fiona jumped and snatched her hand back, her cheeks heating at having been caught holding hands with a man in public.

"Please order thyself something," Caleb said.

Fiona racked her mind. She wasn't actually much for coffee, and there was no telling whether the tea here would be any good. Then she remembered what Caleb had told her the day they first met.

"The drinking chocolate, please." She smiled at Caleb. "I hear it's delicious."

Caleb grinned, clearly remembering as well, and ordered the same. The drinks took only a few moments to arrive, and Fiona smiled as she took the first creamy sip.

"Oh, this is divine," she said. She took another sip, letting the smooth sweetness roll over her tongue. "I think this is the best drinking chocolate I've ever had."

"I would never fib, and certainly not about chocolate," Caleb said. His eyes lingered on hers a moment longer than was customary before he said, "What did thee wish to speak with me about?"

Right. She'd asked him here for a reason.

"Being the light, I suppose."

Caleb straightened in his chair when she used his words, and she smiled, pleased to be able to capture his interest so intently. If they weren't busy with their drinks—and if they weren't in public where anyone might see, of course—she'd take his hand again.

"Tell me more." Eagerness percolated through his voice.

"I have an idea for the children for Christmas." She paused for effect. "A concert in the Smithsonian lecture room on Christmas Eve."

Caleb beamed back, his entire face radiating joy. "They will be delighted. Martha, especially. She tells great stories of the concerts her parents used to give. Who will be performing?"

Fiona laughed. "*They* will. I heard them singing in the yard when I came to return your handkerchief. They're wonderful! And Martha could accompany them on our piano. I've already spoken with Secretary Clark, and he loves the idea. He even suggested we offer free admission and ask the attendees to bring small gifts so the children will have presents to open the next morning."

Caleb's face fell, and he swallowed hard, his Adam's apple bobbing, before he spoke again. "I am so sorry, but I cannot accept."

All Fiona's glee drained from her body, a balloon with the air let out. Not once had it occurred to her that Caleb wouldn't be thrilled by the idea. "Whyever not? There would be no cost at all to the home beyond the time the children spend rehearsing. And think of how much the home could gain. The Institution's events attract Washington's elite. Congressmen, businessmen, men with money to donate to charities. Not to mention the gifts for the children."

Caleb looked down into his mug and took a slow sip of his chocolate, clearly searching for his next words.

"I cannot express how grateful I am that thee went to such trouble on behalf of the children," he said at last, "but Friends don't celebrate Christmas."

Fiona stared at him, her eyes blinking rapidly. "Are you sure? I thought that was Presbyterians."

Caleb chuckled ruefully. "I cannot speak for the Presbyterians, but I assure thee, Friends don't celebrate Christmas. We believe every day is equally sacred unto the Lord, that we should celebrate the Messiah's birth every day, so we don't single out Christmas Day as special." He shrank in his seat. "And we also don't use any music in our worship."

Fiona stared at him again, wishing she'd researched the Religious Society of Friends before ever suggesting this idea. "You don't even sing hymns?"

Eyes downcast, Caleb shook his head.

Somewhere deeper in the café, a man's curse was immediately followed by the sound of a cup shattering on the floor. Fiona was certain that if she glanced over, she'd see the shards of her grand designs for a Christmas concert scattered over the floor, just waiting to be swept up and tossed out with the refuse.

At last she swallowed a hard knot that had risen in her throat and said, "I suppose that's that, then."

Caleb turned his head and watched their waiter sweep up the broken cup a few tables away. He gnawed on his lower lip, clearly deep in thought. Not wanting to interrupt his concentration—and hopeful that when he spoke again he'd have good news—Fiona stayed quiet and sipped the last of her drinking chocolate. She savored every luscious drop in case this meeting ended disappointingly, in which case, she wasn't certain she'd ever be able to bear returning to this café, no matter how good the chocolate was.

After what felt like an entire geological age, Caleb turned back and met her gaze again.

"There may yet be a way," he said. "Let me speak with my Meeting tomorrow. They will help me discern."

Fiona felt a little flicker of hope reignite in her heart.

Chapter Six

Jacob stared at Caleb incredulously, his mouth gaping open like a beached fish.

"Let me get this straight," he said. "An intelligent, *unmarried* young woman asked you to help her organize an event, which presumably would require you to meet with her alone several times, and you said *maybe*?"

Caleb grimaced. It sounded terrible when Jacob put it like that. "Yes?" he said tentatively, raising the end of the word in a question.

Jacob stopped packing his tools and bottles into his leather doctor's bag and beckoned to Caleb.

"Get over here. I need to examine your head."

Had Caleb been Spryly's age, he would have stuck out his tongue at his friend. As it was, he rolled his eyes skyward.

"It would have been dishonest not to explain to her that we don't celebrate Christmas. At least not to the extent that most do."

"Then for the love of all that's holy, Caleb, come up with an alternative idea!"

Caleb waved his hands to shush him. Jacob's rising voice would echo through the entire house, and the last thing he needed was for the children—especially Spryly—to think he was involved with a woman. The boys would barrage him with a never-ending stream of embarrassing questions and sly remarks, while the girls, likely led by Martha, would start planning a wedding.

"I've already resolved the situation. I spoke with the Meeting yesterday, and we agreed that there is no reason not to allow the children to perform the concert, if they wish. They aren't Friends, and many Meetings have been softening on the idea of celebrating Christmas over the past couple years anyway. Besides, it will be good for the community's morale. Perhaps hearing the children sing about the birth of the Messiah will remind everyone to be kinder toward their fellow man."

He'd been relieved when the Meeting lit up at the idea of the children performing at the Smithsonian. Fiona's offer had been so kind and generous and clearly driven by love that the thought of turning her down had broken his heart. He didn't want Martha to lose the opportunity to play a piano again, and selfishly, he worried that saying no to Fiona might mean never having cause to see her again.

He smiled, remembering her soft hand in his, and the way her dark eyes sparkled with excitement as she told him her plan. She was intelligent, certainly, and she was also beautiful. She left him wanting to know everything about her—her family, her favorite book, how she managed to become the head librarian at the Smithsonian, what her dreams were for the future.

"Yoohoo!" Jacob snapped his fingers in Caleb's face, making him jump.

"Sorry." Caleb shook his head to clear it. "What was thee saying?"

Jacob chuckled. "I said I'm glad you got it sorted out. If she's as smart and pretty as she must be to get your mind wandering away like that, you need to spend more time with her." The amusement on his face shifted to a serious expression, and he walked over and closed the door to the parlor, which he used as an examination space whenever he visited the home. "We need to talk about Spryly."

The usual coziness of the room vanished, and Caleb felt doused by a sudden chill. "What about Spryly? He seemed fine this morning." The boy hadn't been quite as perky as usual since his last round of bronchitis, and Caleb had been trying to convince himself that it was due to the chilly, damp weather they'd been experiencing. Everyone moved a little sluggishly when the weather started its slow turn toward winter.

Jacob sighed. "He's not exactly ill, but he's not as healthy as he should be, either. He's still wheezing, and he should have shaken that by now. How's his appetite been?"

Caleb shrugged. "The same as ever, I suppose. I'm not with the children at every meal, but Regina hasn't mentioned anything to me about Spryly not eating his share."

"That's good, at least," Jacob said, nodding. "I just don't like the sound of that wheeze."

"Perhaps he simply needs more rest."

"What he needs is to get out of this city." Jacob pinched the bridge of his nose. "The air here from that damn canal…" He looked up, his gray eyes brimming with sadness. "It's going to take him from us, Caleb."

Jacob's curse tolled like a funeral bell in Caleb's head. The chill that had washed over him a few moments ago now seeped into his bones. He couldn't lose Spryly. He'd never be able to bear losing another child. And certainly not the curly-headed little puck who had wormed his way into everyone's hearts. He reached into his pocket and fingered the embroidered handkerchief.

"What would thee have me do?" he asked, fighting to keep his voice from cracking. "I can so rarely place a child with a family, even within the city. I've made inquiries into a placement for him in the country, but with all the uncertainty right now, my search has yielded no fruit."

Jacob laid a hand on his shoulder and gave him a reassuring squeeze. "I know how hard you've tried. I've asked around, too, and haven't had any luck either. But I've had another idea."

A little of the tightness crushing Caleb's chest loosened. "Which is?"

"My brother."

"In California?" Caleb had only heard tell of William Carter. By the time Caleb met Jacob, Will had been in California five years, he and his family making up four of the hundreds of thousands of people who rushed out there in '49. Unlike most Forty-Niners, though, Will had actually made a fortune, just not in gold. He'd started a cattle ranch to feed all the miners and now owned some thirty thousand acres outside Placerville.

Jacob nodded. "He and my sister-in-law always wanted more children than the two they have, and I think Elizabeth may be past the point for them to have hope of a third. They'd love him like their own, Caleb. He'd get to grow up riding horses with two older brothers through that clean, fresh air."

Caleb tried to imagine Spryly on horseback. More likely, the boy would slip away with the horse's oats before the poor beast knew what had happened. He'd spent years breaking Spryly of his pickpocketing habit, and every once in a while, the child would still turn up with a coin or two in his pocket, leaving Caleb suspicious that he hadn't been entirely successful.

But he *could* imagine little Spryly running free through tall grass, with sunshine on his face and clean air pumping through strong lungs. Sending him all the way to California would almost certainly mean they'd never see each other again, but he'd much rather say farewell to the boy at a train station than at a funeral.

"Has thy brother agreed to this?"

Jacob shook his head. "I wanted to talk to you first, make sure you were all right with the idea. But I don't expect Will to turn me down. If I write to him tonight, we should have his answer by Christmas."

The home would never be the same without Spryly—his own *world* wouldn't be the same without Spryly—but Caleb ran a fingertip over the handkerchief once more, a reminder that there were much worse possible outcomes.

"Please write the letter."

****

Busy teaching the children, Caleb couldn't get away to see Fiona again over the next couple of days. He wanted to tell her in person that the children would perform the concert, but he hated to leave her in suspense. On Fourth Day, he hired a messenger boy at the post office to deliver a note letting her know he had good news and would come by the library late in the afternoon on Sixth Day.

The messenger had disappeared around the corner before Caleb thought to wonder if he should have said "Friday" in his note instead of "Sixth Day." Nothing to be done about it now, he thought. And he had faith in

Fiona's ability to figure out what he meant.

He couldn't stop smiling when the boy returned a few hours later with a note from Fiona saying she looked forward to seeing him again.

After lunch on Sixth Day, he told the children he had to step out to arrange a surprise for them and left them in Regina's care. He could walk the three miles to the Castle in well under an hour, so he should arrive early enough to speak with Fiona for a good long while. Hopefully the library wouldn't be busy today. Much as he wanted to spend time with Fiona, he couldn't monopolize her and keep her from assisting other patrons.

He'd almost caved in and told the children about the concert, but he decided he should grant Fiona that honor. The concert had been her idea, after all. Still, he could hardly wait to see the looks on the children's faces, especially Martha's.

When Caleb reached the Castle, he had to stop himself from breaking into a run and sprinting to the library. He couldn't deny he was eager to see Fiona again. Jacob was right—he'd been insane not to accept her offer immediately. She was intelligent and kind and beautiful, so much so that he'd had trouble focusing at Meeting on First Day. Every time he tried to center down, an image of Fiona's dark eyes and pale skin waltzed through his brain.

And now he was about to arrange to see her many times over the next couple of months.

He strode into the library with his heart singing, and when Fiona turned and their eyes met, she broke into a radiant smile.

"Caleb," she said. Her voice echoed through the

library, and she clapped a hand over her mouth, her eyes widening in horror. Next to her, the library's clerk, Nicole, snorted.

Nicole took a small stack of books from Fiona's hands as Caleb approached. "I'll put these back. You take care of the gentleman here." Her eyes danced with suppressed laughter as she tilted her head to Caleb in greeting and swept away with Fiona's books.

Caleb whipped off his gloves and lightly clasped Fiona's outstretched hand. A tingle traveled up his arm so robustly that if someone had attached a wire to his head, they could have used him to send telegrams.

"Fiona, so lovely to see thee again. If not for the calendar telling me otherwise, I would think it had been far longer than six days." A burst of pride swelled in his chest. He'd never known he could be such a smooth talker.

Fiona giggled, a bright sound like a small bell.

"I agree with that sentiment," she said, a hint of pink rising in her cheeks. She cleared her throat and glanced around, as if suddenly remembering she was in the middle of the library she oversaw. "Shall we step into the reading room? It will be a more comfortable place to sit and chat, and I don't think we have many patrons there right now."

She led him out of the library proper and into the West Range, which boasted rows of tables and racks of newspapers and scientific and literary journals. Only two men were there, both of them paging through newspapers.

"Miss," one of them said as Fiona and Caleb walked past, "I'm finished with this." He thrust the newspaper at her as if she were a tavern keeper and he was finished with his beer. Caleb caught the slightest flicker of Fiona's gaze skyward before she plastered on a tight smile and took it from him.

"Thank you, sir, I'll put this away for you," she said. The man rose and strode out of the reading room, never knowing that Fiona's eyes were shooting icy daggers after him the whole way.

Caleb's jaw tightened. "He shouldn't treat thee like the help."

Fiona shook her head. "It's a daily occurrence, I'm afraid. But it's no matter. At the end of the day, his tax dollars help pay my salary, so the joke's on him."

Caleb chuckled and took the newspaper from her. "Please, let me put this away." As he walked toward the closest newspaper rack, he caught a glimpse of a headline on the front page: "John Brown to hang for treason." He sighed. The slaveholders were going to make an example of Brown, and the abolitionists were going to get a martyr. The situation didn't bode well for peace. He slung the paper on the rack as quickly as he could and hurried back to Fiona.

She'd sat at one of the tables, and he settled into a seat opposite her, their positions reminding him fondly of their meeting at the café last week. He'd been so relieved when she'd ordered the drinking chocolate, freeing him up to do the same. He didn't admit it to many people—being a Quaker already marked him as odd to most of society—but he detested coffee. Nasty, bitter beverage that no amount of milk or sugar could improve. Not to mention it made him antsier than Spryly.

"So," she said, "I'm eager to hear this good news of yours."

Caleb grinned and told her of the Meeting's decision

to proceed with the concert. Fiona cheered softly and clapped her hands in the most delightful display Caleb thought he'd ever seen.

"Oh, I was so hoping they'd agree," she said. "What did the children say when you told them?"

"I haven't told them yet." He glanced down at the table, afraid that gazing into her eyes would make his next statement sound too pleading. "I was hoping perhaps thee would like to join us for supper tonight, so thee could tell them thyself. It was thine idea, after all."

When he lifted his gaze again, he saw Fiona sitting there with her mouth in a perfect "o" of surprise.

"Gracious," she said. "I'd certainly love to, and I hate turning you down for supper twice, but my family will worry if I don't return home after work."

"I'll send them a message!" Nicole's voice rang out from the next table, and Caleb and Fiona both jumped. Caleb clutched his chest. When had Nicole come in?

Fiona whipped her head around and glared at her clerk. "Shouldn't you be shelving books?"

Nicole ignored Fiona's question and approached the table. When she spoke, she addressed Caleb. "She'd love to join you tonight. I will ensure her family doesn't worry."

Chapter Seven

When Nicole intervened, Fiona's cheeks had grown so hot with embarrassment that she'd thought she might burst into flame. But the sensation quickly turned to gratitude as it sank in that she'd be spending the evening with Caleb.

She hadn't been able to shake him from her thoughts ever since he'd taken her hand at the café last week. The warmth of his skin against hers, the reassurance that traveled straight from him to her. The drinking chocolate was divine, but she would have given it up if it meant the waiter had never come by, causing her to snatch her hand back to preserve appearances. She shouldn't allow herself to be interested in a man, but her heart ached at the thought of not being near Caleb as often as possible.

Now she found herself sitting opposite him in a cab as it bounced along the streets toward Georgetown. She'd told him she could walk the distance—in the company of a man, she'd be safe—but Caleb wouldn't hear of it, saying she'd been on her feet all day and he wouldn't dream of making her walk all that way in the chilly evening air. She hadn't wanted him to spend the money—the director of an orphanage couldn't possibly earn much—but now that she was enclosed in this small space with him, catching whiffs of homemade soap, she was glad he'd insisted on the cab.

They didn't speak as they crossed over the canal

bridge and onto Pennsylvania Avenue, but now and again their eyes met and they smiled at each other. Caleb had such a lovely smile, soft and kind and genuine. She hated to pry—she always tried to leave her research at the library door—but she desperately wanted to know more about this softhearted man who loved children. As they bumped along past the President's House, she opened her mouth to ask him where he was from, but she was interrupted by the cry of a newsboy on the sidewalk.

"John Brown to hang December second!" he called out, his adolescent voice cracking on the last syllable.

Fiona cringed. Her heart had plummeted this morning when the library received its delivery of the day's papers and she'd seen the headlines. Hanging John Brown would do nothing to heal the nation's rift over slavery, and it didn't even seem to be much of a punishment for the man. The newspapers reported that in his speech to the court a couple days ago, he'd offered himself up as a martyr to the causes of justice and abolition. The situation was certainly going to get worse before it got better.

Fiona groaned inwardly and looked up at Caleb, hoping he hadn't heard the boy too. But the look in his eyes when they met hers told her that he had.

"Horrible," he said.

She nodded. "I fear what happens next. What will become of us if—" She broke off, worried her voice might break.

Caleb held her gaze and lifted his eyebrows as if in a question. Fiona stared at him, trying to understand what he was asking. He nodded to the empty space on the seat next to her, and a thousand butterflies took flight in her stomach.

She mustn't let him sit next to her. He would get the wrong idea about their relationship. Besides, she barely knew him. They'd not spent half a day together, all told, and a good portion of that had been amid a sea of children. And she could *not* get involved with a man.

She nodded and scooted closer to the leather wall of the cab to make space for him.

She inhaled deeply as he slid onto the seat next to her, detecting the slightest hint of shaving soap on his skin. She studied his jawline out of the corner of her eye and smiled. She liked that he was clean shaven rather than sporting one of the thick, bushy beards that were popular now, some so intricately sculpted they were better described as topiary than facial hair. She had a theory that men wore them to hide weak chins. In that regard, Caleb certainly didn't need a beard. His chiseled jawline flowed cleanly into a strong chin. The urge to trail a finger down that jawline hit her so hard that her hand started to itch, and she clasped it firmly with the other to avoid giving in to temptation.

Caleb reached up and rested his index finger lightly on the side of her jaw farthest from him. Her skin prickled under his touch. With gentle pressure, he turned her face toward his.

"We will continue to be the light," he whispered, his voice barely loud enough to be heard over the horse's clopping footsteps and the hubbub from the street.

Fiona's breath caught, her lips parting as she stared into the deep green sea of his eyes. Even with the cab's curtains pinned up, no one could see in very well as they rolled past. All she had to do was lean forward a hair's breadth. She had no doubt he'd understand the invitation.

But she couldn't, no matter how strong his chin or

how green his eyes.

"Like a Christmas star," she said and turned her head to face forward once more.

Caleb shook his head as if coming out of trance. "Yes, uh, certainly." He stared straight ahead, too, and for a few moments, they rode perfectly parallel to one another, a pair of stone statues.

But Fiona couldn't abide it very long. As they crossed through Foggy Bottom and approached Rock Creek, she let her right hand slide from her lap and come to rest, palm up, on the worn upholstery of the seat between them. Out of the corner of her eye, she saw Caleb's eyes widen as they flicked to her hand, then back up again. And then, oh so slowly, his hand slid into hers.

Her fingers wrapped instinctively around his, and even through her glove she could feel the warmth of his skin, that same reassurance she'd felt when he took her hand at the café. She let out a long, slow breath, tension flowing out of her, and relaxed against the seatback.

When she finally allowed herself to glance at him, she saw him gazing at her, a smile tugging at the corners of his mouth.

****

Fiona beamed as several of the children shrieked with glee upon discovering her in the dining room when they came in for supper. Martha ran up and gave her a hug, while Spryly executed a deep bow—punctuated by a rattling cough, Fiona noted with a frown. Whatever illness he'd had certainly seemed to be hanging on. Curse the air in this town. She blamed it for the fever that claimed her brother's life two years ago. Such a terrible idea to build a city in a swamp.

Caleb must have noticed Spryly's cough, too,

because he put an arm around the boy's thin shoulders and led him to a seat at the table. He then pulled out the chair at the head of the table and beckoned Fiona to take it, settling himself at the foot after she was seated.

"Well, Fiona," Caleb said after a moment of silence which he'd encouraged everyone to use for reflection on their gratitude for the meal, "perhaps thee would like to tell the children what brings thee to our table this evening?"

Fiona looked at the twelve eager faces shining at her like stars and smiled. The rest of the country may be afire, but here in this cozy house was joy. Christmas was nearly six weeks away, but she could already feel its gladsome tendrils reaching toward her.

"I have spoken with Secretary Clark at the Smithsonian, as well as Mr. Fox—er, Caleb—of course," she began, feeling odd referring to Caleb by his first name to the children, "and we have all agreed that you children shall perform a Christmas concert at the Castle on Christmas Eve."

The children stared at her, mouths agape, for several seconds before all bursting out with questions at once.

"How'd you talk him into it?"

"What songs will we sing?"

"Will there be actual *people* listening to us?"

"But I thought Quakers didn't celebrate Christmas?"

"I don't gotta wear a tie, do I?" This last from Spryly.

Fiona caught Caleb's eye and laughed.

"One at a time, please," Caleb said, waving his arms in a downward motion to quiet the children. "First, the Meeting has decided that the concert is in the best interest of you children and the community at large."

Several children opened their mouths again, but Caleb waved them down once more. "Second, yes, there will be people listening. And third, Spryly, thee does have to wear a tie."

"And Martha," Fiona said, turning to the young teenager sitting on her immediate right, "I was hoping you'd accompany the children on the piano. I would, of course, make sure you have plenty of opportunities to come to the Castle to practice."

To Fiona's absolute horror, the girl burst into tears.

Fiona looked across the table at Caleb, who looked every bit as surprised and bewildered as she felt. He made to rise from his chair, but she gestured to him to stay seated and turned to Martha.

"I apologize," she said. "I shouldn't have assumed you'd want to play. You certainly don't have to. There are plenty of pianists in the city. One message to the churches in the area, and we'll have more than we know what to do with, I'm sure."

Martha shook her head so hard a tendril of hair came loose from her braid. She opened her mouth, then shut it again, clearly unable to get any words out. Instead, she jumped from her seat and threw her arms around Fiona's neck, pulling her into a tight hug, the girl's tears dripping onto the high collar of Fiona's dress.

"Thank you," Martha sobbed into the lace. "Thank you."

Through some sort of maternal instinct she'd never been aware of, Fiona wrapped her arms around Martha and held her tight while her sobs slowed.

"My apologies," Martha said when she'd composed herself and took her seat. "It's only that I haven't had the opportunity to play for three whole years. Not since

Mother and Father…" She bit her lip and drew in a deep, shaky breath. "I don't think you have any idea how much this means to me." Fresh tears streamed silently down her freckled cheeks.

Fiona's heart broke. Three years. This child had lost her parents when she was ten, the same age Fiona had been when her own mother died. Her father had died seven years earlier—Fiona had no memory of him—and if not for her older sister Susan, who had been twenty at the time, Fiona might have ended up in an orphanage herself. Her mind flooded with images of all the opportunities she might have missed, the books she might not have had access to, the love she would have ached for. These children had Caleb and Regina, but it couldn't possibly be the same as having a home with one's own family.

She looked around at the eleven other children at the table—Spryly, Eric, Patricia, several whose names escaped her at the moment—and a strange, hot surge of an unfamiliar emotion coursed through her. When she instinctively reached out and took Martha's hand and felt the girl's delicate fingers, not yet at their adult length, squeeze back, she realized it was protectiveness.

Protectiveness and an urge to do…*something*. This concert was a good start, but it wasn't nearly enough. She ached to give these precious children something more.

If only she knew what.

She'd have to dwell on that a while. In the meantime, they had a concert to plan.

"I take it this means you'd like to play the piano for the concert?" she asked.

Martha giggled through her tears and nodded. "Except I haven't got any music."

Fiona smiled. "Lucky for you, I'm a librarian."

Martha's eyebrows shot up. "Do you think I could get more books from the library when I come to practice?"

Fiona glanced at Caleb, who nodded vigorously, a wide smile lighting up his face.

"You certainly may," she said.

Martha sighed wistfully. "You're so lucky to spend your days surrounded by all those books. I wish I could work there."

"Perhaps someday you can. More and more women are entering the field. Why, my own clerk is a woman, though she's leaving soon to be married."

"I suppose you'll have to hire a new one," Martha said.

"I suppose I shall."

She'd been putting off replacing Nicole because she couldn't bear the thought of her dear friend no longer being at her side every day. But Martha was right. She had to hire a new clerk. The library was growing so busy she'd actually be well served hiring two, though she was certain she'd never get the budget for that. She understood now why her brother George had been so eager to bring her on as his apprentice.

Apprentice.

The epiphany crashed into her like a runaway horse. Good gracious, would Secretary Clark go along with the idea? She couldn't see why not. He'd be doing a good turn *and* saving the Institution a great deal of money. Her mind churned with details, each raising new questions of its own. But surely she could work it all out. She knew enough people near the Castle, and particularly over in Capitol Hill, where she and her family lived. Perhaps…

No, Susan likely wouldn't care for that. Their house was full enough as it was. But she could work it out. She knew she could.

"Fiona?" Caleb's voice snapped her out of her thoughts. "Could thee please pass the butter?"

"Oh," Fiona said, casting about wildly for the butter before finding it directly in front of her plate. "My apologies. You've caught me woolgathering."

In her mental absence, the children had dissolved into a cacophony of chatter about the concert—what songs they hoped to sing, how many people they thought would attend, whether Caleb would finally understand about Christmas.

Caleb scrunched up his face in mock indignation at this last suggestion. "I understand perfectly well about Christmas," he said. "I just, historically, have not celebrated it. But," he said with a sly smile at Fiona, "perhaps I shall have to learn how."

Chapter Eight

Caleb grinned as he escorted Jacob's daughter, Lyddie, along with Martha into the Castle a week later. Fiona had asked him to give her a few days to find the sheet music Martha would need and to determine a time when they could get her into the lecture room to begin practicing on the piano. Martha would teach the children their singing parts *a capella* at the home like she'd always done, with one or two dress rehearsals in the Castle prior to the concert, but she herself needed access to the piano to practice.

Jacob had brought Lyddie with him on his last visit to the home a few days ago, and when Lyddie heard they were going to the Castle so Martha could play the Institution's Steinway, she begged to come along. She'd been taking piano lessons herself for several years but had only ever played on uprights, and the Smithsonian's square grand piano was too great a temptation to be silenced by even Jacob's sharpest reprimands about not inviting herself on other people's outings.

Trying not to laugh at his friend's struggle with his child, Caleb pulled Jacob aside and said he'd be happy to take Lyddie along to the Smithsonian if Jacob could collect the girls in his buggy at the end of Martha's practice session. As usual, Jacob caught on immediately.

"Hoping to spend some time alone with a certain librarian, are we?" he asked, wiggling his eyebrows.

Caleb narrowed his eyes. "My business is my own."

Jacob snickered but agreed to pick up Martha and Lyddie.

Now, as Caleb led the girls into the library, he was surprised to see a tall, gray-haired man standing next to Fiona at the desk.

"Mr. Fox," Fiona said, striding up to him, her hand outstretched. Caleb's eyebrows jumped. *Mr. Fox?* Whoever this man by the desk was, he must be important.

"Fiona Ellicott," he replied, accepting her handshake. "I don't know if you've met Jacob Carter's daughter, Lyddie." He gestured to Lyddie. "She's a good friend to us at the home, and she expressed interest in seeing the lecture room."

Fiona smiled at Lyddie and shook her hand. "Lovely to meet you," she said, then turned to the older man, who had drawn up alongside her as they spoke. "Secretary Clark, may I introduce Mr. Caleb Fox, director and head teacher of the Friends' Home School in Georgetown. Mr. Fox, this is Secretary Alexander Clark, director of the Smithsonian Institution."

Stunned silent, Caleb fought to temper his astonishment. Fiona hadn't mentioned anything about meeting the director of the entire Smithsonian. Thanks only to his childhood training did he automatically extend his hand.

"A pleasure to meet thee, Alexander Clark," he said. "I hadn't expected to see the Institution's director today."

If the secretary was insulted by Caleb's omission of his title, he didn't show it, letting out a chuckle instead. "Neither did Miss Ellicott. I admit that I sprang myself on her. By happy coincidence, I glanced at the lecture hall's schedule this morning and saw you were coming in. I simply had to meet the man in charge of our Christmas Eve concert."

Caleb felt his cheeks flush. "Oh, I'm hardly in charge." He smiled. "The concert was Fiona's idea, and I'm not much for music."

Behind him, one of the girls—Lyddie, from the sound of it—snorted. He ignored her and continued.

"Directing the children and accompanying them on the piano will be handled by Martha Dalton here." He gestured for Martha to step forward. She took one shy step toward Alexander Clark.

"A pleasure to meet you, sir." Her voice was hardly louder than a church mouse, but she extended her hand to the secretary, who clasped it warmly.

"The pleasure is mine, Miss Dalton. I do hope you'll enjoy playing our Steinway. I know my own daughters have taken great delight in it."

At this mention of daughters, Martha smiled up at the man, her face now blooming with confidence.

"Thank you, sir," she said. "Oh, this is my friend, Lydia Carter. I hope you don't mind that she joined us today. Her father is a physician in Georgetown. He tends us when we're ill."

Lyddie extended her hand as well and gave the secretary's a hearty shake.

"Lovely to meet you as well, my dear," he said, clearly genuinely delighted by the young ladies. "And on that, shall we say, note?" The secretary chuckled at his own joke. "Let us proceed upstairs so you can see the grand instrument for yourself." He offered one arm to Martha and the other to Lyddie and led them out of the library, leaving Caleb and Fiona behind.

Caleb turned to Fiona, hoping he looked more self-assured than he felt. Unexpectedly meeting the head of the Smithsonian had thrown him completely off balance, even worse than the one and only time he'd attempted sailing.

"Shall we?" He offered her his arm. She smiled and slipped her hand around his arm with an air of familiarity. He grinned, pleased that she felt so comfortable with him. As they headed toward the stairs in the South Tower, he tried not to get too distracted by her. But she wore the same light-gray dress she'd worn the day he brought the children to the museum, and her hair, swept back into a loose bun at the back of her head, smelled faintly of lavender. He was heady in moments, fighting the urge to bury his nose in her thick locks and inhale deeply.

"Here we are," she said.

Caleb glanced around, realizing they were now on the second floor and having no memory whatsoever of climbing the stairs. Alexander Clark and the girls waited for them in front of a heavy wooden door.

"Did you visit the lecture room with the children?" the secretary asked.

"No," Caleb said, proud of himself for finding his voice despite his utter befuddlement over being so close to Fiona. "We spent so long in the apparatus room that we ran out of time."

The secretary chuckled again, and Caleb guessed that many guests got caught up in the apparatus room, and for good reason. The children had marveled at the gadgets in there, especially Hare's Electrical Machine which was mounted on one wall and generated static electricity that it transferred to whomever sat in the chair beneath it. Little Patricia's hair had stood on end for a good ten minutes after she gave it a try, and all the children had laughed until tears leaked from their eyes.

"You are in for a treat." Secretary Clark threw open the door with a flourish. "Mr. Fox, ladies, welcome to the Smithsonian's lecture room."

Caleb sucked in a breath as he took in the enormous, fan-shaped hall with its towering ceiling. When Fiona had said "lecture *room*," he'd imagined something simple, more along the lines of his meetinghouse on Massachusetts Avenue, maybe with a lectern at the front.

This was most assuredly *not* like the meetinghouse.

"The architects originally planned the lecture room to be on the first floor," Alexander Clark said, "but I felt it would be better up here. No columns obstructing anyone's view of the speaker's platform." He stamped a foot on the polished wooden platform on which they stood.

"How many people can fit in here?" Lyddie asked. Caleb followed her gaze up to the balcony at the far end of the room and thought her question quite astute.

"Fifteen hundred comfortably," Alexander Clark said. "Two thousand if they don't mind squeezing in."

"Two *thousand*?" Martha said, her eyes like saucers.

"Don't worry, they'll all be able to hear you," Alexander Clark said, misunderstanding the question. Caleb could tell Martha was nervous at the thought of that many people watching her perform, not astonished that the hall could hold so many. "This room works like the bell of a trumpet. We're at the mouth, as it were, and the fan shape, combined with the high ceiling, amplifies the sound. Even those guests sitting all the way in the back row at the top of the balcony can hear the speaker just fine."

"Well," Martha said, "I suppose I'd better get practicing, then." Her voice trembled so slightly that Caleb suspected he was the only one who noticed, and his chest swelled with pride over his young charge's courage.

"Please enjoy the piano," Alexander Clark said. "I must get to a meeting with a young scientist who wishes to conduct some exciting experiments with electromagnets." He rubbed his hands together, more excited than Caleb was used to seeing a man of the secretary's age and stature, and he decided that he liked this man a good deal. Caleb and the girls bid the secretary farewell and thanked him for the brief tour.

When the door closed behind the museum director, Fiona turned to Caleb, Martha, and Lyddie.

"Caleb, Lyddie, please feel free to take seats anywhere in the hall. Martha, why don't you get started? The music is already on the piano for you." She pointed toward a gleaming grand piano on the opposite side of the stage.

Martha's dark eyes welled with tears, and she groped next to her until she found Lyddie's hand and clasped it tightly. Together, the girls made their way across the stage, where Martha reached out one trembling finger and traced it lovingly along the shining rosewood. A little sob escaped her lips, and Lyddie pulled her into a hug.

"They'll be with you in every note," Lyddie said, and Caleb felt hot tears sting the corners of his own eyes. Lyddie's mother—Jacob's beloved wife—had died four years ago of Bright's disease. The Friends' home had opened only a year later, and Jacob had immediately answered the call for a physician who could tend the children. Caleb saw no coincidence there. Left to raise his daughter alone, Jacob held a special place in his heart for motherless children. And clearly, Lyddie felt a comradeship with them as well.

Martha nodded and took her place at the piano bench, Lyddie settling in beside her. "To turn pages," Lyddie said, but Caleb knew it was so Martha felt less alone when she sat at a piano for the first time in three years.

"I'll be down in the library if you need anything," Fiona said close to Caleb's ear, her breath prickling the skin on that side of his neck. It was now or never.

"Might I take thee to dinner when we're finished? To thank thee for all thee has done for us?"

He'd guessed Fiona would accept, but it was still a relief when her face broke into that radiant smile that made all his cares burn away like fog in the sunshine.

"I'll look forward to it," she said. "It's the opposite direction from Georgetown, but there's a lovely restaurant in a little hotel in Capitol Hill, not far from my home. I'm sure the girls would love it."

Caleb couldn't stop the smug smile that stretched across his face. "Lyddie's father is coming to collect the girls in two hours. Dinner will be just the pair of us."

Fiona's eyes sparkled. "In that case, I shall look forward to it even more."

Chapter Nine

Fiona smiled as she locked the library door at the end of the day. Nicole had headed home ten minutes ago after no shortage of sly comments and nudges in Fiona's ribs when she learned that Fiona was having dinner with Caleb.

"It's simply an act of gratitude for me arranging the concert," Fiona insisted, but Nicole only snorted and looked away, pretending to sort some books.

Now, as the bolt clanged into place and a hard jiggle ensured the door was secure, Fiona bit back a grin. Ever since Secretary Clark had approved her newest plan a few days ago, she'd been dying to get another chance to speak with Caleb privately. She didn't want to say anything in front of Martha in case he disapproved. But something told her he'd be excited.

She stepped out of the Castle and into the crisp November air. Winter certainly was on the way. They didn't usually get snow until much later in the season, but she hoped they'd have some for Christmas. There was something magical about fresh snow on the ground on Christmas Day. The children would love it. She spotted Caleb standing near one of the young trees on the other side of the little road that curved in front of the building.

"Ready to go?" he asked when she reached him. His words came out with a little white puff of breath.

Fiona nodded and slipped her gloved hand through the crook of his arm, glad that she'd worn her nicer pair today.

"Which direction?" Caleb asked. "I don't often come into the city."

Fiona nodded her head east and led them around the building to B Street. "The hotel is just over a mile from here."

They walked the two blocks to Maryland Avenue in silence, Fiona wondering how to bring up her offer for Martha. She was certain Caleb would agree, but her stomach twittered with nerves anyway. She'd never been very good at starting conversations. As a librarian, she was used to people approaching her with questions, so she rarely had to worry about it.

After thinking hard, she finally spoke. "Do you like the carols I selected for the concert?"

Caleb smiled and looked at her. "I do. Music has never been much of a part of my life, but I look forward to learning these songs."

"Carols are one of the nicest parts of Christmas. If you're going to learn how to celebrate the holiday, they're an excellent start."

Caleb paused and directed them to one side of the sidewalk to allow a pair of ladies to pass. Senators' wives, most likely, this close to the Capitol. Or their mistresses. When they set off again, Caleb adjusted Fiona's hand on his arm, drawing her a little closer to his side. Her shoulder nearly brushed his, and she was glad she hadn't adopted the wide skirts so many women were wearing now. They were beautiful, but she worried she wouldn't fit between stacks of books at work. And now they would have served only to distance her from Caleb.

When they reached the bridge over the canal, she was doubly glad not to be wearing a voluminous skirt. All that fabric and crinoline would have slowed her pace, and she would have had to smell the fetid stench longer. She bit back a giggle when she realized that Caleb was holding his breath, too, as they crossed the bridge. He might not come into the city often, but he clearly understood about the canal.

"Jacob suggested I read Dickens's *A Christmas Carol* as well," he said when they were safely on the other side and striding toward the Capitol Building.

Aghast, Fiona stopped dead.

"You've not read *A Christmas Carol*?" Dickens's little Christmas book was one of the most popular titles at the library. She remembered the year it was published. She and George had heard so much about it that they checked their favorite bookstore every day for two weeks until they spotted a copy. "Spryly is a veritable Tiny Tim, and you haven't read it?"

Caleb smiled sheepishly. "Spryly's always brought the Artful Dodger from *Oliver Twist* to my mind. I love Dickens, but…" He shrugged.

"But Friends don't celebrate Christmas," Fiona finished.

Caleb chuckled. "Though I hear we're starting to."

Fiona laughed and they set off again, soon passing directly by the Capitol Building, its roofline leveled off since the old dome had been removed a few years ago. Work had stalled last year, thanks to arguments between the architect and the engineer in charge of construction, but with the appointment of a new engineer, the newspapers sounded hopeful that the new dome would be finished soon. Fiona certainly hoped so. The building looked out of place without its top, like a man wearing only half a hat.

They continued along Pennsylvania Avenue, Fiona hoping Caleb would say something more that she could use to segue to the opportunity she had in mind for Martha, but he offered nothing. A sigh escaped her lips before she could stop it.

"Something on thy mind?"

Fiona cringed inwardly. This wasn't how she'd wanted to go about this, but nothing for it now, she supposed.

"Martha, actually."

Caleb turned his face toward her, one eyebrow cocked. When he didn't reply, she continued.

"She loves the library. And with Miss Daly getting married next month, I find myself in need of a new clerk."

Now it was Caleb's turn to stop dead in his tracks. He stepped in front of Fiona and studied her face, seemingly oblivious to the people grumbling as they had to step around them to continue along the sidewalk.

"What is thee suggesting?"

Fiona grabbed his elbow and shuffled them into the doorway of a bookshop that had already closed for the evening.

"I spoke with Secretary Clark again," she said, unable to contain her smile. Why in the world had she been nervous about broaching this subject? "He's agreed to allow me to train Martha as my apprentice, just like my brother trained me. He'll even pay her a little. Not much, mind you, but enough to cover her cab fare to and from Georgetown, and a little extra to jingle in her pocket. I'd originally hoped to find somewhere she could board close to the Castle, but this is even better." In truth, she couldn't quite believe it. The secretary was a kind man, but she had never expected him to do this much.

Caleb stared at her and swallowed hard, making his Adam's apple bounce. Fiona struggled to interpret his expression. He didn't look upset, but he didn't look happy either. He just looked...stunned. Her heart sank. She'd overstepped. She must have.

"I apologize," she began. "I suppose I should have spoken to you first—"

Caleb pressed his index finger to her lips, silencing her. An emotion rose in his brilliant green eyes that she couldn't quite place. Some odd mixture of joy, sadness, and...relief?

"Thee cannot possibly understand how much this means to me." He blinked hard several times. "And what it will mean to Martha." He took off his hat and ran his fingers through his hair. He opened his mouth again just as a woman—an adventuress, judging by the dangerously low cut of her tight bodice—leaned against the doorway they stood in.

"Hey there, fella," she crooned, running her eyes up and down Caleb. "Why don't you leave the schoolmarm here and come along with me? I'll show you a *much* better time."

Even in the shadows of the doorway, Fiona could see the color rise in Caleb's cheeks, and judging by the heat creeping up from under her collar, she was sure hers were doing the same. She drew in a deep breath and straightened to her full height, ready to chase the harlot off, when Caleb reached into his pocket and drew out a silver half-dollar. He pressed it into the woman's hand.

"Have thyself a hot meal and a quiet night," he said

gently, looking the woman straight in the eyes.

In that moment, Fiona truly saw the woman. She passed sporting women nearly every day going to and from the Institution. Her eyes registered their presence, but she'd never really *seen* any of them.

Because she'd never bothered to look at them like Caleb did just now.

Hot shame burned the tips of Fiona's ears as she took in this woman, who, now that Fiona studied her, proved to be quite young, not yet out of her teens. Her face was pale under her rouge, and her dark eyes, which should be vibrant and full of life, were hollow and empty. A hard lump rose in Fiona's throat.

At the same time, the girl burst into tears, choked out a "Thank you, sir," and hightailed it down the street and out of sight. Fiona stepped out of the doorway and watched her go, then turned back to Caleb.

"That was most kind of you," she said, unable to bear looking him directly in the eyes. But she caught the sad smile that crossed his expression.

"I know I cannot save them all, yet I still try."

Fiona nodded, somehow knowing that when Caleb said "them," he didn't mean only the fallen women of Washington City but all the lost souls who crossed his path. She chuckled ruefully.

"It would seem, Caleb Fox, that you understand far more about Christmas than you think you do."

Chapter Ten

Caleb glanced around the hotel lobby and smiled. He'd worried at first that Fiona was leading him to some opulent hotel whose restaurant was favored by congressmen, but he felt right at home in the cozy space inside the John Hancock Hotel.

Unlike the famous founder's signature, the hotel that bore his name was unassuming, its three stories composed of plain red brick on the outside and modestly furnished inside. Caleb and Fiona stepped into the little restaurant, dimly lit with gas lamps that flickered against dark red wallpaper. The maître d' led them to a small table in a corner, where Caleb helped Fiona with her chair. He took his time making sure she was settled, enjoying the extra moment to breathe in that faint scent of lavender that seemed to follow her everywhere.

Caleb had never been to a restaurant with a printed menu before, and he delighted in seeing his options listed before him. How the children would love this! He chuckled, imagining Spryly tucking a napkin into his collar and demanding the "biggest piece o' pie you got back in that kitchen."

His chest ached a little at the thought of Spryly. Would Jacob's brother have received the letter yet? Caleb calculated in his head. No, it had only been ten days since Jacob said he'd write to Will. Even if he'd written the letter that night and posted it the following morning, it certainly wouldn't have made it all the way to California yet. Like Jacob had said, they likely wouldn't receive a reply until close to Christmas.

"Now something is on *your* mind," Fiona said, smiling slyly at him from across the table. Her hair shone in the lamplight, and Caleb realized he'd never met a woman so beautiful as Fiona Ellicott. He found himself thinking of her in the evenings after the children went to bed. How he'd love to have her there to pass a few peaceful hours chatting or reading at the end of the day. They'd known each other only a few short weeks, yet he had trouble sometimes remembering what life was like before he'd met her. Jacob had been right. He'd been an absolute fool not to say yes to the Christmas concert idea immediately. Thank goodness the Meeting had talked him into it.

"I was thinking of Spryly, actually," he said.

She smiled her beautiful, brilliant smile. "How is our dear little urchin?"

The ache in Caleb's chest tightened, and his expression must have changed because Fiona's smile faded.

"He's all right, isn't he?" Her voice trembled ever so slightly, and Caleb's chest tightened another degree. It was clear that even in only a few short weeks, Fiona had grown to care for the children, and he knew what he was about to say would break her heart as much as it had broken his. He ran a hand down his face.

"He's recovered from his bronchitis, but his lungs are weak. Jacob said that if he stays in the city…" He couldn't bring himself to finish the sentence. If he didn't say it aloud, maybe it wouldn't come true. He bit his lip and looked down at the creamy white tablecloth.

"Oh, Caleb."

A soft, warm hand covered his where it rested on the table. Caleb looked up and saw Fiona's eyes reflecting the same sadness he was certain shone through his.

"Is there anything to be done?" she asked.

He nodded. "Jacob has written to his brother in California in hopes he might take the boy." He told her what he knew of William Carter and his family. "Jacob expects he'll agree, and I must remember how grateful I am for that."

"You can be grateful that he'll be somewhere he can grow up healthy and still be sad about having to say farewell to him," Fiona said softly. "It's not contradictory."

Caleb shook his head in wonder. How had Fiona known the exact feelings he'd been grappling with?

"I thank thee for that."

He wanted to say more—so much more—but the waiter came by just then to take their orders and Fiona snatched her hand away. They both asked for the oyster pie, which Fiona assured Caleb was a specialty here. When the young man shuffled off, Caleb searched his mind to find the thread of what he'd been wanting to express before the interruption.

"I suppose," he said at last, "that even after being in this position for a few years, it is difficult for me not to be able to save each and every one of them myself." He cocked his head. "Does thee suppose that's pride?"

Fiona smiled. "No. I think that's having a big heart. At least," she said with a light laugh, "I hope that's what it is. Because I have to admit, from the moment I met them, I've wanted to save them too. Especially Martha. She reminds me so much of myself as a girl, always dreaming of something more, something bigger." She glanced down. "It made me realize how fortunate I was to have my family to care for me. My parents died when I was still a girl, but my sister Susan went to work so our brother George and I could stay in school. He's the one who trained me as a librarian. Ever since he died two years ago, I suppose I've been looking for a way to carry on that legacy. And Martha's the perfect age to begin an apprenticeship."

"She is," Caleb said. "And I should have apprenticed her out already, but after what happened with Ruth last year..." He stuck his hand in his pocket and fingered the embroidered handkerchief.

Fiona wrinkled her brow. "Who's Ruth?"

Caleb sighed, knowing he was bound to answer her truthfully, even if he'd rather not. He looked down and spoke to the tablecloth.

"She was one of my charges, about a year older than Martha. I hired her out to a shopkeeper when she turned thirteen. She was brilliant with a needle and thread, but I failed to find a seamstress or tailor willing or able to take her on. I could tell she was disappointed, but she didn't complain. Ruth never complained. And she had her own room in the little apartment over the store, so she was content."

He paused and took a long sip of his water, gathering his courage to relay what happened next without weeping. He was generally against crying in public, particularly in front of beautiful women. And a few other patrons had given him sidelong glances when he and Fiona had walked in. Likely, they'd spotted his wide-brimmed felt hat with its short crown—a telltale sign of a Quaker. Today's Friends didn't endure the persecution of their ancestors, but Caleb knew that many people still found them odd. He was grateful it didn't seem to be a problem for Fiona. And somehow that fact made it a little easier to get out what he said next.

"The owner was a kindly older gentleman, and he and his wife treated her well. But they were getting on in years and couldn't move around as easily as they once had. One afternoon, the wife started to fall. Ruth caught her but lost her own balance." He drew in a deep breath and let it out slowly. "She fell into a display of glassware and cut her arm deeply. But Ruth being Ruth, she didn't complain. She didn't want the lady to feel bad, so she wrapped her arm up herself and didn't let on that anything was wrong, even when it got infected. By the time the shopkeeper realized she was ailing and sent word to me, there was nothing Jacob could do. The infection had spread to her heart. Even amputating the arm wouldn't have saved her."

Fiona exhaled. "That poor child."

Caleb looked up and saw tears welling in the corners of Fiona's eyes. "I know it wasn't my fault, but it's made it difficult for me to let any of the children go, even the lucky few who find families." He pulled the handkerchief out of his pocket and passed it across the table to Fiona. "Ruth made this for me a few months before she died. I know it isn't plain, but I can't bear not to carry it. It was such a beautiful gift. *She* was such a beautiful gift."

Fiona traced a finger along the bright stitching. "No wonder it meant so much to you to get it back."

Caleb nodded and reached across the table for her hand. "And it means a great deal to have the friendship of someone who cares so much for the children. I cannot thank thee enough for all thee has done for them."

Fiona squeezed his hand. "And you'll never have to."

****

Even though Fiona's house was the opposite direction from his, Caleb insisted on walking Fiona home after dinner. They'd enjoyed a wonderful meal and even more delightful conversation. Having grown up in the city, Fiona had expressed great interest in his childhood on a farm, and he kept her laughing with tales of sheepherding gone awry.

She was interested in Quakerism, too, and peppered him with questions on the walk home.

"Do you really sit in silence for hours?" she asked.

Caleb smiled. Being quiet was one of the most difficult aspects of Quakerism for non-Friends to grasp.

"Our forebears would sit for hours, but my Meeting typically worships for only an hour. And it is not always silent. Often a Friend will feel led to speak."

"About what?"

He shrugged. "Whatever God has revealed to them."

Fiona fell silent herself then, and Caleb guessed she was probably working out how to ask him about some other difficult aspect of Quakerism for non-Friends to grasp. They strolled under the yellow halo of a streetlamp, and Caleb waited expectantly for her to speak to him.

"Do you *truly* believe that women are equal to men?" she asked, all in a rush.

He stopped, turned toward her, and took both her hands in his, wishing they weren't separated by the gloves they both wore. She met his gaze, and her lips parted ever so slightly, inviting him to stare at them. His heart picked up speed, and he took a deep breath.

"I do. *We* do." He squeezed her hands and released her, setting off down the sidewalk again. "Everyone is imbued with the spark of the Divine. Man, woman, child, Black, white, Indian, everyone. Women have full equality within the Meeting, and typically within the home." He chuckled. "A fact which my mother frequently reminds my father."

Fiona laughed too. "That explains why your people were so involved at Seneca Falls and now with abolition."

Caleb nodded. "We aren't faultless. Friends were enslavers once too. But it gladdens me to see so many of our number working for atonement."

They walked along in silence for another block or so, Caleb wishing they'd never reach Fiona's home and have to say goodnight. He wanted more time. He *needed* more time. He couldn't find the words to tell Fiona how much her arrangement for Martha meant to him, but maybe if they just kept walking, she'd be able to sense it somehow, like when truth was revealed to him during worship. He'd never met another woman like her—smart and beautiful and curious.

No, that wasn't right. He'd met smart and beautiful and curious women before. What he'd never met was a woman who was smart, beautiful, and curious about *him*. And his children, for that matter. He'd met a few women over the years who thought it sweet that he worked with orphans, but none of them had ever even visited the home, let alone gone to the lengths Fiona had to make the children happy.

How had no man yet claimed her? Though Fiona Ellicott didn't strike him as a woman capable of being claimed. She had a will and a mind of her own, and she wasn't afraid to wield both. If she fell in love, it would be because she chose to.

What might prompt her to choose him?

True, they'd known each other only a few weeks, but in that time, she'd shown him her intelligence, her compassion, and her... What was the phrase? *Joie de vivre*. He desperately wanted to be a part of it.

Marriages between Friends and non-Friends, while not encouraged, were no longer unheard of. His Meeting had readily agreed to the Christmas concert. Perhaps they'd accept a marriage to a non-Friend, especially someone as interested in Quakerism as Fiona seemed to be.

"This is it." Fiona's voice jarred him out of his thoughts, and he looked up at a narrow, three-story rowhouse. A haze of yellow lamplight crept around the curtains on the front windows. Fiona slid her hand from his arm and turned to face him. "Thank you for walking me home, and especially for dinner tonight. That was most kind."

Caleb smiled. "'Twas the least I could do. Thee has been kinder to me and mine than I ever would have expected."

Fiona smiled back, her eyes crinkling a little at the corners. "Do not think you can take advantage of my kindness, sir. I expect to see Martha at the library bright and early Monday morning."

Caleb chuckled. "I shall ensure she arrives promptly at eight."

They stood there for a moment, just smiling at each other, and Caleb stared again at Fiona's lips, so full and alluring. He merely had to lean forward a few inches to brush them with his own. Fiona took a tiny step forward, narrowing the already slim gap between them. His blood pounded in his ears, making it hard to think straight. All he could focus on was Fiona's face—her nut-brown eyes, upturned nose, and those heavenly lips. The city could vanish around them, and he was sure he wouldn't notice. He inhaled, ready to lean in and press his lips to hers, but then hesitated.

What if Fiona wasn't interested in a romantic relationship with a Quaker? Was this Friend merely a friend to her, so to speak? He had to find out before he flung himself at her. It wouldn't be fair to her otherwise. He took a small step backward while he tried to determine how to go about finding out.

"Caleb?" Fiona said, her brow wrinkling. "Is everything all right?"

The idea descended on him so fast and hard it might as well have been flung down at him from Heaven. He grinned.

"Would thee like to accompany me to Meeting tomorrow morning?"

Fiona's head jerked back. Whatever she'd been expecting him to say, this clearly wasn't it. But as he suspected she always did, she recovered quickly.

"I'd love to, but unfortunately, I promised my niece I'd help her with some sewing tomorrow."

His smile faded from his lips. "Thee must keep thy promise."

"But I could go next week."

His grin reappeared so fast and so wide it made his cheeks ache. "Next week it is," he said, nearly choking on the laughter that was trying to bubble up from his chest. "Meeting starts at nine o'clock, so I'll come for you about eight?"

Fiona laughed lightly. "I'll be ready."

"Then for now, my dear lady, I bid thee a fond farewell. May the week pass quickly until we see each other again." He bowed low and kissed the back of her gloved right hand.

Fiona laughed again. "Goodnight, Caleb."

"Be well." Giving her hand a final squeeze, he turned and headed down the sidewalk.

"Caleb?" Fiona called after him. He turned back. "I wasn't joking. I expect to see Martha first thing Monday morning."

Her laughter carried him down the sidewalk, and he knew he'd hear it echoing in his dreams.

Chapter Eleven

Martha arrived at the library Monday morning, a whirlwind of blue calico, dark plaits, and excited chatter. She thanked Fiona at least two dozen times before she'd made it all the way through the library doors.

"I couldn't believe it when Caleb told me I'd be working at the library," she said breathlessly. "And not just any library, the *Smithsonian*! I get to play the piano and teach the children their songs and work at the *Smithsonian*!"

The girl kept on in this manner for so long that Fiona had to remind her to breathe. When Martha had inhaled several times, Fiona introduced her to Nicole.

"This is Miss Daly. She'll be leaving us in a couple of weeks, and while she's still here, she's going to teach you her duties so you can take over."

Martha's eyes shone with a swirl of elation and astonishment. "I'm going to be your *clerk*?"

Fiona caught Nicole's gaze and stifled a laugh. "Perhaps someday. For now, you're my apprentice. Learn everything Miss Daly has to show you, and in a few weeks, I'll teach you some more."

"Come along, my young charge," Nicole said, putting her arm around Martha's shoulders. "Allow me to introduce you to the library catalog. Miss Ellicott compiled it herself, you know." Nicole babbled away about the catalog and shelving as she led Martha toward the desk.

Over the course of that week, Martha spent her mornings with Nicole and the afternoons with Fiona learning about cataloging, shelving, and acquisitions. If the lecture room upstairs was free at some point during the day, Fiona would send Martha upstairs for an hour or so to practice the piano. On Thursday, the girl said the other children were already catching on to the Christmas carols, and she couldn't wait to bring them into the Castle for a rehearsal on stage. Fiona promised she'd reserved the hall for them the mornings of the second and third Saturdays in December.

"It's so funny to hear someone say 'Saturday' and 'Sunday' and the rest," Martha said. "After three years with Caleb and Regina, I've started thinking of the days of the week by their numbers."

"Why do the Friends do that?" Fiona asked, realizing that was one question she hadn't thought to ask Caleb last Saturday.

"The names for the days of week come from pagan gods, so they won't use them," Martha said with a little shrug. "They do the same thing with the months."

"Prepping for Meeting on Sunday, are we?" Nicole asked with a snicker as she passed behind them, balancing a tall stack of books in her hands. Fiona resisted the sudden urge to reach out and poke the stack to make the volumes tumble to the floor. But she couldn't bear to risk damaging the books, and it would probably set a bad example for Martha.

Martha's eyes widened. "You're coming to Meeting?"

A tingling sensation raced down the back of Fiona's neck like she'd sat under Hare's Electrical Machine upstairs.

"Caleb invited me, and I thought that it would be nice to join you all since we've become such good friends." She smiled, pleased with herself for that response. Martha beamed, clearly pleased too.

"Dr. Carter says that Friends make the best friends," she said.

Fiona laughed. "That they do."

****

Sunday morning, Fiona tapped her foot nervously on the wood floor as she peeked out the parlor window for at least the fourteenth time.

"Are you quite well?" Susan's voice bounced across the room, making Fiona jump.

"Yes, quite," Fiona said.

Susan smiled and crossed the parlor, joining her at the window. "It's only a quarter till," she said. "I'm sure he'll be here right at eight o'clock like he said he would." She took Fiona's gloves, which Fiona had been twisting mercilessly into little leather balls, and smoothed them out. "It's good to see you stepping out with a man. I do hope you'll invite him back for dinner. I'd like to meet this Caleb of yours."

"He isn't *mine*," Fiona insisted, snatching back her gloves. "I haven't the time for that sort of nonsense. He's merely a friend." She smiled, remembering Martha's quip about Friends making the best friends.

Susan clearly misinterpreted her smile. "Of course he is," she said with a smirk.

Fiona looked up and met her older sister's gaze. "You know I can't let him be more than that."

Saying it aloud pained her. She knew she growing fond of Caleb, fonder than she should allow herself to become, but she couldn't help it. He was kind and charming and, no need not to admit it, exceptionally handsome. She saw his enticing green eyes every time she closed her own. She'd thought he was about to kiss her last week when they said goodnight outside her home, and cold disappointment had flushed through her when he hadn't. She hadn't seen him since then, and she'd had to tell herself not to count down the days until today like a child waiting for Christmas morning. The thought of Christmas made her smile again, and she glanced toward her handbag in which she'd secreted the little gift she planned to give Caleb after Meeting.

Susan's smirk softened into a fond smile. "You might yet. If there's one thing I know about my younger sister, it's that she can find a solution to any puzzle." She leaned forward and kissed Fiona's forehead, and Fiona melted a little. Her sister had stepped right up as a mother to Fiona when their own mother died, and even now that they were adults, Susan always seemed to know exactly the right words to make everything better.

A knock on the door made them both jump.

"Gracious, that's him!" Fiona said. She dashed to the settee and snatched up her handbag while Susan answered the door.

"Greetings," Caleb said. Fiona turned just in time to see him doff his hat and smile at her older sister. "I've come to collect Fiona for Meeting."

"She's right here," Susan said. "Do come in." When Susan turned to clear the doorway for Caleb, her eyes were wide and she mouthed, "Oh my!" at Fiona. A giggle bubbled up in Fiona's throat, and she barely tamped it down before it escaped. She was glad her brother-in-law had stepped out this morning and wasn't home to see

Susan agape over a handsome man stepping into the parlor. Or her, for that matter.

And there he was, Caleb Fox, director of the Friends' Home School in Georgetown, standing in her family's parlor, being just as handsome as he could be. He clasped his hat in front of him, and Fiona bit her lip when she saw he was wearing the same plain coat and trousers he always wore. She'd agonized for nearly an hour last night over what to wear this morning, finally settling on her favorite green silk. It was a fine fabric but without too many ruffles or too voluminous a skirt, and the fact that it matched Caleb's eyes had absolutely nothing to do with her selection whatsoever. Now she worried she was overdressed. Would her gown mark her as an interloper? Perhaps she should have gone with the plain black dress she'd worn while in mourning for George. She'd considered it last night but had ultimately tucked it away in the back of the wardrobe, the reminder of her brother's passing too painful to shroud herself in.

Caleb sucked in a breath when his gaze settled on her, and he hesitated a moment before stepping forward. Fiona's heart sank. She was overdressed, for certain, the shock evident in Caleb's aghast expression. But then he took her hand in his and smiled.

"Thee looks lovely."

Fiona hadn't yet pulled on her gloves, and her bare hand tingled under his touch. She smiled back, so relieved she was speechless. She stared at him until Susan cleared her throat and Caleb stepped back, releasing Fiona's hand.

"We should depart if we wish to be on time," he said.

Fiona nodded, tucked her handbag under her arm,

and pulled on her gloves. Then, taking Caleb's proffered arm, she bid her sister farewell and headed out the door.

****

Though Caleb's reaction to her dress had helped set her at ease, Fiona still breathed a sigh of relief when she stepped into the Friends' meetinghouse and saw that most of the other women were dressed similarly. Their fabrics were fine, but their gowns unadorned with the usual ruffles and lace.

She and Caleb hadn't spoken much on the almost two-mile cab ride that Caleb had insisted they take from Capitol Hill. Shortly after leaving her house, they'd passed a newsboy on the street hawking a headline about John Brown's execution next week. Fiona shuddered. Seemed every day had more headlines than the last about the visitors Brown received at his jail cell in Virginia and the letters he wrote. Even if she weren't a librarian seeing a dozen newspapers a day, she wouldn't have been able to evade the news; the whole city was abuzz over it. Rattled, she hadn't been able to come up with a pleasant topic for conversation.

Without thinking, she scooted an inch or two closer to Caleb on the cab seat. He must have bathed last night because she could detect the faint aroma of lye soap on his skin, and his jawline was so smooth he must have shaved just that morning. Fiona fought the desire to pull off a glove and run a finger along his jaw. She might not be able to help growing fond of him, but she could at least refrain from caressing him in public.

Caleb turned his face toward her just then and smiled. Wordlessly, he took her hand in his, twining their fingers together, and held on to her for the rest of the ride.

Now, as they settled onto a bench in the

meetinghouse, Fiona wished he'd hold her hand again. But they were in public now—at Meeting for Worship, of all places—and such a display would be improper. If she hoped to make a good impression, she probably shouldn't paw at the man who brought her.

She'd been to church only a few times in her life, most recently her brother's funeral two years ago, but the meetinghouse was unlike any church she'd been in. Rather than facing toward an altar, two banks of pews faced the center of the room, and Fiona noticed none of the usual trappings. No crosses, no ornate candlesticks. Just a few dozen plainly dressed people greeting each other warmly. And a handful of familiar children, of course.

Fiona smiled to see Martha, Spryly, and the rest file in. Caleb had said the children weren't Quaker, but apparently they came along to Meeting anyway. That was likely for safety, now that she thought about it. Regina and Caleb couldn't very well leave Spryly to his own devices every Sunday morning while the rest of them came to Meeting. Goodness only knows what they'd return home to. A chimney-sweep conglomerate operating from the front porch, or possibly a menagerie milling about in the parlor. Fiona bit back a giggle as she noticed everyone around her sliding into the pews. She settled herself next to Caleb and waited.

As if by some unspoken signal, the entire Meeting drew in a deep breath, let it out slowly, and fell into silence.

Fiona closed her eyes but had no hope of ever quieting her mind as Caleb had instructed. Her thoughts drifted to the newsboy they'd seen along the way hawking news of John Brown's upcoming execution.

She'd read the other day about militia assembling in Charles Town, where Brown was imprisoned. Rumors of both a lynch mob and a rescue mission had swirled, and tensions were high, even in Washington City. There was just so much hate and violence that Fiona felt almost overwhelmed at times. In this country, where supposedly "all men are created equal," were men ready to tear each other apart to prove their superiority. Her stomach clenched, as it so often did these days, a physical manifestation of the high-strung emotions all around her.

But then, a funny thing happened. Next to her, she felt and heard Caleb draw in another deep breath and let his exhalation linger. It distracted her just enough that she could take stock of the people around her. Even without opening her eyes, she found she could sense them all. Caleb on her left, Regina on her right. In the pew in front of them were the children. One of them was fidgeting, and she was sure it was Spryly. When she cast her mind out a little farther, she felt the presence of all the other Friends, a warm, comforting sort of feeling. The world was in turmoil outside, but inside this meetinghouse, all was peaceful.

The tension in her shoulders relaxed, and all thoughts of executions and war faded from her mind, and she lost herself in the stillness. Suddenly, she felt Caleb slip his hand into hers. Startled, she popped her eyes open and smiled, squeezing his hand affectionately. Only when he tilted his head and raised one eyebrow did she realize he was shaking her hand, not being sly. Around her, she saw the other Friends shaking one another's hands, breaking their silence. Her cheeks burned. Meeting must be over. It didn't seem possible, but the entire hour had passed. She let go of Caleb and turned to shake Regina's hand.

A few moments later, everyone took their seats again while a few members made announcements, including, to Fiona's surprise, Martha, who reported that the children's choir rehearsals were progressing nicely and that she hoped everyone could attend the concert on Christmas Eve.

The announcements finished, Caleb introduced Fiona to at least a dozen people whose names she had no hope of keeping straight, and then led her outdoors. After the peaceful coziness of the meetinghouse, finding herself back on Massachusetts Avenue in the middle of Washington City felt like falling through the ice on a frozen pond. She shivered.

"Is thee cold?" Caleb asked, glancing up at the sky, which was unusually clear and bright for mid-November.

Fiona shook her head. "It's just jarring, going from in there to out here."

Caleb grinned. "That it is. Happens to me every week." He chewed his lower lip for a moment. "Did thee find it agreeable?"

Fiona felt her eyebrows lift. "Agreeable? That was wonderful. I can't recall the last time I felt so serene."

Caleb pressed his right hand to his chest, over his heart. "Truly?"

Fiona nodded, unable to contain a wide smile. The look of surprise and tempered hope on his face was the sweetest thing she'd ever seen.

Caleb's grin reappeared, lighting up his whole face. "Would thee like to come again? Perhaps next week?"

In that moment, she would have walked to the moon if he'd asked her. Instead, she nodded. "I'd love to."

Unlike the ride earlier, on their journey in the cab back to Fiona's house they chattered the whole way, talking about the children's progress with their songs, Martha's work at the library, and a scheme Caleb had overheard Spyrly and Eric concocting to talk their way into the President's House and get hired as butlers. They laughed nearly the entire ride, and by the time they reached the Capitol Hill neighborhood, Fiona had forgotten that she'd ever been upset this morning.

Caleb helped her out of the cab outside her house and walked her to her door, Fiona taking her steps as slowly as possible without being too obvious. Even though she'd get to see him again next Sunday, she didn't want him to leave yet. She should have agreed to Susan's suggestion that she invite him in for dinner, but she couldn't spring an unexpected guest on her sister now. Susan would have the meal nearly prepared already.

As she climbed the final step to the door, her handbag thumped against her leg, and she smiled, remembering the gift she carried for Caleb. She might not get to see him again for a week, but at least she'd send him off with a little reminder of herself.

"Shall I collect thee the same time next week?" he said, turning to face her.

Her heart soared. "That would be lovely. And next week you must come in for dinner after. Susan would love to get to know you, and you haven't met Michael or the girls at all yet."

"I would enjoy that." He gazed into her eyes as if he were searching for what to say next but couldn't find the right words. Not wanting to miss an opportunity, Fiona spoke up.

"I hope you'll enjoy this too." She reached into her handbag and pulled out the brown-paper-wrapped package she'd carried since he picked her up. She held it out, and he stepped a bit closer and took it from her, a quizzical little smile tugging up one corner of his mouth.

"What is it?"

Fiona giggled. "Open it."

"Thee has left me no choice, I suppose." He chuckled and pulled a penknife from his pocket. He sliced the twine and pulled away the paper to reveal the small book inside. He stared at the cover for a moment, then read, "*A Christmas Carol, in Prose: Being a Ghost Story of Christmas* by Charles Dickens." He burst out laughing, and Fiona joined him, warmth gushing through her at his delighted reaction to her gift.

"Promise you'll read it," she said when their laughter tapered off. "You'll learn so much about Christmas, and if Tiny Tim doesn't remind you of Spryly, I'll eat my hat."

Caleb grinned, slipped the book into his coat pocket, and took hold of her hands. He gazed intently at her and took another step closer. "I promise," he said, his voice suddenly husky. Fiona's heart sped up, and she took a tiny step closer to him. Desire radiated off him like it had after their dinner a week ago when she'd told him of Martha's apprenticeship. Fiona knew she shouldn't encourage him, but she couldn't help it. She smiled shyly, hoping he'd get her silent message.

He did. Sliding one hand around her waist, he pulled her to him, pressing her body against his. Even through his coat, she could feel his warmth as she wrapped her arms around him.

She hadn't been kissed in nearly ten years. Kissing

could lead to falling in love, which could lead to marriage, which would *certainly* lead to the end of her librarianship. But as Caleb pressed his soft, full lips to hers, she could no longer deceive herself.

She had fallen in love with Caleb Fox, and there was nothing she could do about it.

Chapter Twelve

Caleb sighed contentedly as he settled into the worn armchair in the home's parlor on Fourth Day afternoon. Martha and the children were upstairs in the large classroom, rehearsing their Christmas songs, and after that they'd play outside in the yard for a while before supper. He had the next couple hours all to himself.

He smiled and ran a hand down the smooth cover of the book Fiona had given him. He hadn't planned to kiss her after Meeting, but after how much she'd enjoyed worship and then given him a gift, he'd been so overcome by hope and—may as well admit it—*love* that he couldn't stop himself.

And Fiona certainly hadn't seemed to mind. He closed his eyes, remembering the feeling of her body against him, her soft lips pressed to his. There could be no doubt now that she was agreeable to a courtship with a Quaker. He would have to bring the matter before the Meeting, though not next First Day. He couldn't very well mention it in front of Fiona. It would have to wait two weeks. But after everything Fiona had done for the children and how she'd shown interest in attending, he had no worries that the Meeting would try to dissuade him from a courtship.

He lost himself in a daydream for a moment, envisioning Fiona in the armchair opposite him, reading a book after the children were in bed, perhaps sipping a cup of chocolate.

He sat bolt upright in his chair. *Chocolate*. He'd never given anyone a Christmas gift before, but since Fiona had given him a gift, it was only right to reciprocate. He'd buy her a block of chocolate so she could enjoy a cup of drinking chocolate at home at the end of a long day at the library.

He smiled again, nuzzled into the soft cushions on the armchair, and cracked open *A Christmas Carol*.

He was immediately appalled by Ebenezer Scrooge's stingy, unkind behavior. But he eagerly gobbled up the story and enjoyed watching Scrooge begin to soften as the Ghost of Christmas Past confronted him with his past mistakes. When Caleb reached Stave Three and the Ghost of Christmas Present, he chuckled when Tiny Tim appeared, though not at the child's poor health. He remembered what Fiona had said about Spryly being a veritable Tiny Tim and realized she didn't know Spryly as well as she thought she did. Spryly might be a bit sickly, but he certainly wasn't as well behaved as Tim Cratchit.

The thought of Spryly's health brought on a brush of sadness. The boy was faring all right; his bronchitis hadn't returned, and he'd avoided catching anything else, at least for now. But it was only a matter of time before a reply arrived from Jacob's brother, most likely with instructions for sending Spryly to California.

No use dwelling on that now, he told himself. They still had the concert to look forward to. He wouldn't spoil what time they had left together by wallowing in sadness. He turned his attention back to the book. The Ghost of Christmas Present was soon replaced by a spectral being, shrouded and hooded, drifting along the ground toward

Scrooge. His breath quickening, Caleb gripped the book tighter. The phantom was covered save for one outstretched hand. In his mind, Caleb pictured not a full hand but merely a skeleton of one, pointing forward, leading Scrooge—

"Caleb?"

Caleb shouted and fumbled with the book, which thumped onto the floor. In the same instant, he drew his feet up onto the chair and wrapped his arms around his legs, squeezing himself into a little ball. He glanced wildly around the room, his eyes finally landing on the form of Jacob—Carter, not Marley—standing in the doorway of the parlor. Caleb clutched his chest and tried to catch his breath while Jacob burst out laughing.

Embarrassed, Caleb unfolded and stood, snatching up the book—undamaged, thank goodness—and trying to look like he hadn't just had the wits frightened out of him.

"So sorry," he said, "I didn't hear thee come in."

"You don't say!" Jacob doubled over in a second, even stronger round of laughter.

Caleb pursed his lips into a thin line and waited for Jacob to compose himself. It was a long wait.

"What are you reading that's got you so absorbed?" Jacob asked when his last hiccups of laughter faded. He stepped forward and plucked the book from Caleb's hands. He smiled when he saw the title. "Lyddie and I love this book." He handed it back to Caleb. "Let me guess. The Ghost of Christmas Yet to Come?"

Caleb nodded and rubbed the back of his neck. "Guess I got too caught up."

Jacob chuckled and clapped him on the shoulder. "It's all right. This book will do that to a body. A bit early for a Christmas story, though, isn't it? Lyddie and I don't usually start reading this one together until about a week before."

Caleb shrugged. "'Twas a gift. I promised I'd read it." He gestured toward the window, through which he could see the children playing outside in the yard. "And I have to take advantage of quiet moments to myself whenever I can find them."

"A gift, eh?" Jacob grinned. "Bet I can guess who gave it to you." He peered hard at Caleb's sheepish smile. "Oh dear, you clearly have come down with a serious case."

Caleb's smile dropped and he took quick stock of himself. He felt all right. No headache, scratchy throat, strange rashes. "A serious case of what?"

"Lovesickness, my friend." Jacob nodded sagely. "And there's only one cure. Have you told her?"

Grinning like a fool, Caleb shook his head. He gestured to the armchair next to his, and he and Jacob both sat. "I've only recently admitted it to myself." He hesitated, wondering how much to reveal, then decided Jacob would worm it out of him regardless, so he might as well save them both the trouble. "But we kissed after Meeting on First Day."

Jacob let out a delighted bark of laughter and clapped Caleb on the back. "I knew you had it in you. When do you see her again?"

"She's coming to Meeting with me again next week, and she invited me to dinner with her family after."

Jacob nodded. "Good, good. But there'll be a lot of people around. You need to get her to yourself again."

Caleb laughed. "I'd love to, but I hardly ever get *myself* to myself."

"That's a good point." Jacob furrowed his brow for a moment, then his eyes lit up. "You'll have to invite her over here."

Caleb stared at his friend. Was he joking? He just told him to get Fiona to himself and then he suggested a house full of children? "I'm afraid I don't see how that would help," he said, trying to be tactful.

Jacob leaned forward in his chair and rested his forearms on his knees. "You invite her here to, I don't know, listen to the children sing the songs they've been practicing. She stays for supper. Then you send the children to bed early and the two of you enjoy some tea and conversation here in the parlor. You're not away from the kids, and you get a chance to talk things over with the lady."

Caleb felt a smile spread slowly across his face. Fiona would get to hear the children's progress on their songs *and* he'd have an opportunity to test whether she was interested in their relationship moving forward in a romantic sense. He pointed his index finger at Jacob.

"Thee is quite bright when thee wants to be."

Jacob chuckled. "I do have experience in this area." A sad smile crossed his face as it always did when he alluded to his late wife. Hannah had been gone four years now—she died shortly before Caleb met Jacob—but Caleb knew not a day passed that Jacob and Lyddie didn't miss her desperately.

All the more reason to love someone while he could, he supposed. One never knew how much time one would have.

****

When they arrived at Meeting next First Day, Fiona settled right in next to Caleb on their bench and fell into silence with everyone else as if she'd been doing it all her life. Like last week, Caleb found it hard to focus on listening for God's truth with this exquisite creature breathing softly next to him.

But perhaps Fiona herself was the truth he'd spent so many years listening for.

He yearned to reach over and take her hand, but he didn't dare disrupt whatever truth *she* might be hearing. He hoped that it was about him.

Meeting ended after its usual sixty minutes, but somehow it had never been longer. Caleb knew he was being rude hustling through the greetings afterward, but he was anxious to have Fiona to himself, even if just for the drive back to her home. His stomach spun when he remembered that taking Fiona home meant going inside and meeting her family. He'd never had to be introduced to a woman's family before.

Sweat broke out along his hairline.

Fortunately for his rapidly rising internal temperature, Fiona insisted they walk back to Capitol Hill rather than hire a cab. She said the clear, brisk day was perfect for walking and they'd be sitting again soon enough as it was. He hated the thought of her walking that far—it was nearly two miles—but walking *would* give him more time alone with her than taking a cab. And as soon as she tucked her hand through the crook of his arm and they set off down the street, he knew that walking was the perfect decision.

They strolled in comfortable silence for a block or two, the chilly, almost-December air cooling Caleb down in short order. He relaxed into the stroll, relishing every tipped hat and wish of "Good morning" they received from passersby. A few gentlemen let their gazes linger on Fiona a second or two longer than was customary, and Caleb swelled with pride at this beautiful woman on his arm. He puffed out his chest but almost immediately felt a hot rush of guilt at being prideful and tucked it back in. But he kept his shoulders square and his spine straight. A man could still be happy and confident.

And since he was feeling so good, he decided to go ahead and suggest the plan he and Jacob—well, just Jacob—had concocted. Besides, this could well be the last private moment he'd get with Fiona today. He cleared his throat.

"I was wondering if thee might like to join us for supper some evening this week. The children could perform their songs so thee can hear their progress. Martha is pleased with how they're coming along."

Fiona turned her face toward him, her eyes alight like she'd just won an unexpected prize. Joy surged through him. Jacob's instincts had been spot on, and Caleb thought that since he was getting into the whole idea of Christmas, perhaps he should buy his best friend a gift.

"I'd love to," Fiona said. "Which evening?"

Caleb suggested Sixth Day, thinking that since Fiona worked only half a day on Seventh Day, she might be inclined to stay out a bit later. But she said she was attending Nicole's wedding on Seventh Day and wanted to get to sleep early the night before.

The very sound of the word "wedding" on Fiona's lips made Caleb's heart flutter. He needed to wrap this conversation up quickly because it was getting harder and harder to concentrate on anything practical.

They settled on Fifth Day, the date—December 2—

ringing a bell in Caleb's mind for some reason that he couldn't recall. His head was too muddled with thoughts of leaning in and kissing Fiona again. But he drew in a deep breath and faced forward once more as they continued walking. He wouldn't kiss her here in public. He'd keep their kissing just between the two of them.

All too soon, they reached Fiona's home, and Caleb's stomach jumped. He'd been so caught up thinking about kissing that he'd nearly forgotten they had a destination. His stomach had been starting to rumble on their walk here, but now as he climbed the steps to the Ellicott home, his appetite was replaced by a slight rolling sensation, as if he'd suddenly stepped aboard a boat.

"Don't worry," Fiona said as she grasped the door handle. "They'll love you."

Before he could reply, she pushed open the door and led him into the parlor, calling out to her family that they'd arrived. Her older sister, Susan, whom Caleb had met briefly last week, glided into the parlor, her hand extended. Caleb grasped it and smiled at this woman who looked like a slightly older version of Fiona. She greeted him and passed him to a stocky man of average height with his hair graying at the temples.

"Michael Davis." The man pumped Caleb's hand. "A pleasure to meet you, Mr. Fox."

"Please, call me Caleb," Caleb replied, a statement he repeated twice more as Fiona introduced him to her two teenage nieces.

Susan herded them all into the dining room, where they sat down to a wonderful meal of roast chicken, potatoes, carrots, and biscuits. The family engaged him in easy conversation about his work with the children, and while Caleb didn't know much about banking—Michael's occupation—Fiona's brother-in-law entertained him with a tale of the baseball game he'd watched on his last trip to New York City. Caleb had heard of the sport but had never seen it, and by the time Michael finished his story, Caleb was ready to buy a train ticket to New York City just to experience it. He said as much, and Fiona smiled.

"Perhaps it will spread here to Washington so you don't have to go so far," she said, squeezing his hand under the table.

Michael grunted. "We have bigger problems to deal with first. They're executing that man Brown on Thursday, and I fear it will be the opening salvo of a larger conflict."

Caleb's meal sat like a rock in his stomach. That's why December 2 rang a bell. John Brown's execution. He heard Fiona swallow hard beside him, and he returned the hand squeeze she'd given him a moment ago.

"I'm certain all will be well," Susan said, her bright tone contrasting sharply with the pointed look she directed at her husband. "Who would like some gingerbread?"

Fiona turned to him and smiled, clearly as eager as her sister to change the subject. "We typically have gingerbread only at Christmas, but Susan and I decided to have it today to celebrate the children's upcoming concert. Get us into the spirit, as it were."

Caleb forced his mouth into a smile, and the mood in the room lightened once more. After two helpings of gingerbread, he waddled out of the family's home, certain he wouldn't need to eat again until after the new year. Fiona followed him onto the porch, despite the chilly day, and closed the door behind them.

"Thank you for coming," she said. "I hope they weren't too overbearing."

He chuckled. "Thy family is lovely. I thank thee for inviting me." He took a step closer, closing the space between them so his coat rasped against the shawl she'd drawn around herself. "And I look forward to seeing thee again soon."

"As do I," Fiona said and pressed her lips firmly to his.

Chapter Thirteen

Fiona breathed a sigh of relief when she stepped out of the cab Thursday evening and made her way up the walk to the orphanage's front door. She'd been holding her breath all day, worried that John Brown's execution this morning in Charles Town would spark violence here in Washington. Everyone in town was like brittle paper, and she'd feared the execution would be a lit match.

But fortunately, nothing. According to the reports she received at the library late this afternoon, the 2,000 soldiers and militiamen who'd descended on Charles Town had kept order even right around the gallows. It turned out the people of Washington City, sixty-five miles away, had had nothing to fear.

Now, as she climbed the steps of the orphanage's front porch, she felt almost giddy, both with relief and with excitement over seeing Caleb again. She touched her gloved fingertips to her lips, remembering that moment last week when he'd leaned in and kissed her.

She'd never known that giving a man a book could change a relationship so profoundly.

But even in the week since then, something had shifted. Something about Caleb felt more certain, less…amorphous. She felt the transformation sizzle like electricity between them at Meeting on Sunday. No, *First Day*. She'd fallen into the silence so easily this time, and as she listened to Caleb's soft breathing beside her, she suddenly knew that he was just *right*. Everything about him and their time together was exactly as things should be, like books lined up in perfect order on a shelf.

She paused before she raised her fist to knock on the door, realizing for the first time how odd it was that none of the children had been in the yard to greet her. She wouldn't have let Spryly romp around in this brisk air, but it was strange that Eric or Patricia or some of the smaller children weren't outside. Perhaps Caleb had kept them in today in case of trouble.

She shivered, wrapped her coat tighter around herself, and knocked on the door. The muffled squeals and footsteps racing around inside immediately shifted her thoughts from the macabre. What in the name of heaven was going on in there?

She'd barely completed the thought when the door creaked open, and there stood Spryly in a worn frock coat that was miles too large for him and a top hat that fell over his eyes when he bowed from the waist. Fiona nearly choked holding back her laughter when she saw the serious expression on his little face.

"Good evening, Miss Ellicott. Please, do come in." He stepped back and swept an arm grandly into the hallway. The last six or seven inches of the frock coat's sleeve swung from the end of his concealed hand, and Fiona had to bite back another bark of laughter. Caleb was right. Spryly was much less a Tiny Tim than an Artful Dodger.

Eric stepped up to her as she crossed the threshold. "May I take your coat, Miss?" he said. He, too, wore a faded, overly large frock coat with a crooked cravat peeking out at the neck. Fiona let herself giggle a little now. She hadn't spent a lot of time with the children, but she'd figured out that Eric's feelings weren't likely to be hurt. And she was right. At the sound of her laughter, the boy looked up and grinned. She slipped out of her coat and handed it to him, and he scampered toward the coatrack.

Fiona heard a throat clearing, and she turned her head to see Caleb standing in the doorway to the dining room just down the hall. She was surprised to see him wearing his frock coat indoors. Most men did, at least in public, but he hadn't had it on during either of her previous visits; he seemed to much prefer his shirtsleeves when at home.

His hair glinted in the flickering glow of the oil lamp on the wall next to him—the Friends' Home didn't yet have the steady gas lighting Fiona and her family enjoyed in Capitol Hill—and Fiona could see that he'd slicked it back. Suddenly feeling underdressed in the same practical blue dress she'd worn to work, she took a step toward him and caught a whiff of woodsy aftershave. He'd shaved too. She ached to reach out and caress his smooth cheek, but it wouldn't be proper in front of the children.

Though where *were* the children? Eric hadn't reappeared after taking her coat, and apart from the Artful Spryly hopping around behind her like a puppy, none of the children were in sight. But before she could think about it very long, Caleb reached out and took her right hand, clasping it warmly in his, and all thoughts of the children flew straight out of Fiona's mind.

Caleb stared hard at her, his gaze settling on her lips. Fiona stepped closer, hoping he'd kiss her, hoping they could both lose themselves in this moment. The corners of his mouth twitched into a faint smile, and he slid an arm around her waist.

"We ain't got time for this!" Spryly protested behind her. Fiona jumped away from Caleb, nearly landing on the little boy who didn't seem to notice how close he'd come to being squashed. "Everybody's waitin' in the dining room."

Mopping his brow with a handkerchief, Caleb looked over Fiona's shoulder at Spryly. "Yes, of course." He fumbled trying to put the handkerchief back in his pocket. "Regina worked hard all day preparing a special meal. It would be rude to let it get cold." He crooked his arm. "May I?"

A special meal? Whatever for? She hadn't expected anything beyond the home's usual simple fare. But Spryly had zipped around them and was now dancing in the doorway to the dining room, so she didn't have an opportunity to think about it further.

"Lickety-click!" he said.

Fiona slid her hand through Caleb's crooked arm and let him lead her into the dining room. When she stepped across the threshold, she gasped.

All twelve children—Spryly dashing into place among them—stood around the table in what Fiona presumed were their nicest clothes. Two of the other boys wore too-large frock coats like Spryly and Eric, and Martha had curled her hair into ringlets. She must have helped Patricia, too, because the younger girl's hair was perfectly curled as well. Every little face was scrubbed clean of the usual smudges, and all twelve sets of eyes sparkled up at her.

"Goodness gracious," she said around the hard knot that had risen in her throat. "What's the occasion?"

Martha smiled and stepped forward. "We wanted to

show our gratitude for what a good friend you've been to us."

Her right hand still wrapped around Caleb's arm, Fiona pressed her left hand to her heart. A warm rush of love for the children shot through her, mixed with a pang of sadness for the parents who wouldn't get to watch these beautiful young people grow up. She'd never thought about being a mother, but she'd adopt every last member of this clan if only she could. She slipped her hand from Caleb's arm and opened her arms to Martha.

"Oh, sweetheart, I should be thanking *you*." She wrapped her arms around Martha and held her tightly, a sense of peace settling over her. For a moment, all that existed were her and this young lady she felt so privileged to instruct and to guide. Finally, she looked up at the other children still smiling at her. "Thank you to all of you. You are making this Christmas season very special for me." She let go of Martha and circled the table, hugging each child in turn. When she reached Spryly, he popped up on his tiptoes, getting himself closer to her ear.

"Martha didn't tell you the whole story," he whispered. "We also know Caleb's sweet on you, and we wanted to make him look good."

Again, Fiona had to bite back a snort of laughter. She was tempted to tell Spryly she'd already guessed as much but decided it might cause more of an uproar than her low tolerance for embarrassment could bear.

A warm hand landed on her elbow, and she knew immediately that it belonged to Caleb. She was already so familiar with him.

"Take your seats," Caleb said, smiling, oblivious to the way he'd just made Fiona's insides somersault. "I don't know about everyone else, but I'm hungry."

While Caleb and Fiona sat, Martha, Patricia, and two other girls scampered away and soon returned with Regina, bearing huge, covered dishes. They set them on the table and, with a flourish, whipped off the lids to reveal three roast chickens, mountains of mashed potatoes, three different vegetables, and heaps of biscuits.

Fiona's giddiness ebbed. The home couldn't possibly have much money in its budget. They shouldn't have spent so much on her. She knew one little boy, Elias, had been brought in off the streets only a week or so before she met Caleb. He sat at one end of the table, a little wisp of a thing, still in need of fattening up. She knew Regina made sure he was well fed, but it still felt wrong to enjoy such opulence when this child had been on the verge of starvation only a few short weeks ago. He was a reminder that too many little ones were still out there on the street, scrounging for whatever scraps they could find to feed themselves. She sighed. The city needed to help these children. Hopefully the concert at the Smithsonian would draw more attention to the plight of orphans in Washington.

She cast a quick glance at Caleb, so grateful that he and the Friends stepped in when the politicians couldn't be bothered, like Ebenezer Scrooge at the beginning of *A Christmas Carol*. A shame she didn't know any ghosts who could visit the U.S. Capitol.

Caleb caught her looking and smiled at her, one brow raised as if in a question. She had to turn her gaze away. If she stared at him now, she'd get right back out of her chair and plant a kiss on him here in front of all the children. She busied herself getting the serving started, and before long, everyone had a heaping plate of food. Fiona smiled to see Elias dig in with gusto.

She loved the chaos of a meal with a dozen children. Spryly refused to remove his frock coat and kept accidentally dipping one too-long sleeve in the butter dish. Patricia somehow got gravy in her hair, and a little boy named Howard daubed a spoonful of mashed potatoes on his face and tried to claim Eric had thrown them at him. This last earned a sharply raised eyebrow from Caleb and a quick apology from Howard for not being truthful, even while Spryly congratulated his comrade on a good try.

The whole time, Fiona was keenly aware of Caleb sitting directly next to her on her left. Every time he spoke, she basked in his warm tenor and gentle speech. He was so good with the children. He knew each child's preferences and quirks and seemed to delight in each and every one of them. And when he spoke to her, she couldn't ignore the way her heart fluttered. Her carefree joy from earlier returned, and she let herself get caught up in the gaiety of this delightful ragtag group.

After a dessert of brown betty, which Spryly declared the most delicious thing he'd ever eaten in all his days, the children began taking dishes into the kitchen.

"Leave the dishes for tomorrow," Regina called after them, "and get to the parlor so Fiona can hear thee sing."

Seconds later, the gaggle of chattering children poured out of the kitchen and skittered back through the dining room on their way to the parlor, Regina bringing up the rear and herding them along. Laughing at the pandemonium, Fiona rose from her seat and, taking

Caleb's arm once more, followed them to the parlor.

They settled into side-by-side armchairs while the children shuffled into two crooked rows. Somehow, Spryly ended up in the back, and all Fiona could see of him over Eric's head was the top of his hat. Martha sighed, reached between Eric and Elias, and pulled Spryly forward, knocking his hat over his eyes again. She nudged the much taller Eric into the back row and stepped back, giving one sharp nod of satisfaction.

Martha turned to Fiona and Caleb. "We only have seven songs, but I thought we could maybe read passages from the Christmas story in Luke in between."

Fiona smiled. "That's a wonderful idea. Secretary Clark will love it."

Martha beamed and turned back to her fidgeting choir. She opened her mouth and sang out a crystal-clear "Ahhhhhhhh."

To Fiona's amazement, the rest of the children sang out the same syllable, matching Martha's pitch precisely for a moment before half of them slid up a third into perfect harmony. Before Fiona could express her wonderment, Martha raised her arms, and the children launched into "O Come All Ye Faithful."

For the next half an hour, Fiona fought back tears as the children sang one sweet-sounding carol after another. Halfway through their finale, a hauntingly beautiful rendition of "Stille Nacht," she felt a warm hand close around hers where it rested on the arm of her chair. She turned her head and saw Caleb smiling at her, his eyes glistening like she knew hers must be. She smiled back, losing herself in the moment for the second time that evening, letting her mind and soul be swept up in the music and the gaze of the kind, handsome man beside her.

When the last notes faded, Caleb slipped his hand from Fiona's just before Martha turned back to them, her cheeks pink.

"We'll sound better in the lecture room with the piano," she said, shrugging.

"Sweetheart, you sound spectacular," Fiona said. "A professional choir couldn't have done better."

She looked back at Caleb, and judging from the awe on his face, guessed this was the first time he'd heard the children perform the songs too. His jaw worked up and down a few times before he found his voice.

"I agree with Fiona. I cannot believe how far thee have progressed in only a few weeks."

The children all grinned and nudged each other. Spryly swept his hat off his head and took a bow. Martha's cheeks reddened further and she dropped her gaze to the floor, a wide smile spreading across her face. She traced a pattern on the floor with the scuffed toe of one shoe.

"I thought we might sing 'Stille Nacht' *a capella*," she said.

"I think that's a marvelous idea," Fiona said.

"It certainly is," Regina agreed. Fiona started. She'd been so swept away by the children's singing that she'd completely forgotten Regina was still in the room. The older lady swiped at the corner of her eyes and rose from the settee in the corner. "Now to bed with thee. Singers need their rest."

A collective groan filled the room.

"It's too early," Spryly moaned.

"Thee all knew this was the plan tonight," Regina chided. "Thee got thy favorite dessert in exchange. Now away upstairs."

Clearly trying to set a good example, Martha smoothed her dress and bid Caleb and Fiona a lovely evening, adding to Fiona that she would see her at the library tomorrow. She grabbed Patricia's hand and led her from the parlor. In twos and threes, the rest of the children trickled after them, Spryly still grumbling.

Fiona listened to the clatter of their feet tromping up the stairs and the echo of laughs and squeals, punctuated by Regina's badgering to wash up quickly and get to bed.

Fiona guessed it would be a little while before the children fell silent, but for the first time all evening, she and Caleb were alone. She let her eyes linger on him, admiring the pains he'd taken to brush up his appearance tonight yet thinking how she preferred his plainness—especially the way his wavy hair flopped around of its own accord when it wasn't slicked back.

He caught her eye and smiled. Gracious, how she loved the way the left corner of his mouth curved up just a little higher than the right when he smiled.

"The children sounded spectacular," he said. He ran a hand through his hair, seemingly without thinking, and several locks sprang free and drooped over his forehead, just the way Fiona liked it. "I hadn't any idea they'd come so far. I'm usually planning the next day's lessons while they rehearse."

"They are going to thrill the audience," Fiona said, taking his hand. His smile widened and he squeezed her hand, never breaking their gaze. The air grew thick around them, and Fiona felt pulled to him like he was one of the electromagnets from the Apparatus room. He must have felt it, too, because he tugged on her hand.

"Please come to me." His voice was husky.

He needn't ask her twice. She slipped out of her chair and stood before him. He slid one arm around her waist and drew her onto his lap. His green eyes bore into her as he softly caressed her cheek.

"So beautiful," he whispered before kissing her gently. She leaned into his lips, resting her hand on the back of his neck and letting it slide slowly up into his hair, twining her fingers through his soft, short locks. Caleb sighed softly and his mouth opened, coaxing hers along with it. He slipped his hand behind her head, and—

A titanic crash resounded from the floor above, followed by children's shrieks.

"Confound it, Spryly!" Eric shouted. "You're gonna clean that up!"

Fiona knocked chins with Caleb as they both snapped their gazes toward the ceiling.

"Do you need to go see what happened?" she asked.

Caleb groaned. "I'd rather not."

"Oh, quit fussin' and get me the damn broom!" Spryly's voice tumbled down the stairs.

"Regina!" another boy's voice called out. "Spryly's cursing!"

"Are you sure you don't need to go up there?" Fiona asked. She wobbled on Caleb's lap as he shifted in his seat.

"I'm sure Regina has it well in hand."

Then the unmistakable sound of a child's hacking cough reached the parlor, and Caleb jumped to his feet, catching Fiona just before she toppled off his lap and onto the floor.

"That's got to be Spryly," he said, his eyes wide with concern. "Please don't go. I must check on him, but…just don't go."

"I won't."

Caleb smiled gratefully, then dashed out of the parlor, his footsteps thundering up the stairs only a second later.

Fiona settled back into her abandoned armchair, scooting it back from the warmth of the fireplace. She needed to cool down. The sound of poor little Spryly's sharp cough upstairs almost immediately chilled her, though, and she scooted right back up to the fireplace.

Should she run for Dr. Carter? Would there be anything he could do if she did? She chewed her lower lip. Caleb and Regina had been caring for Spryly for some time now. They'd know if he needed the doctor. She should just sit tight and wait for Caleb to come back downstairs.

Finally, after what felt like hours but was only a couple of minutes according to the sagging grandfather clock in the corner, Spryly's cough eased. Fiona let out a long breath and slumped in her chair, trying to smooth the wrinkles in her skirt from where she'd balled it in her fists.

Another minute or two later, she heard footsteps coming down the stairs, and then Caleb stepped back into the parlor. The rest of his hair had sprung free from its careful combing, and he looked exhausted. She stood and rushed over to him.

"He's all right," Caleb said, taking her into his arms. Relieved, she rested her head on his chest. "I had to give him a dose of whiskey to settle him, but he's all right. For now."

Fiona looked up. "Is he ill?"

Caleb shook his head and sighed. "No more than usual."

"I hope you hear from Dr. Carter's brother soon. Spryly would be much better off in the clean, dry air of California."

Caleb swallowed hard and nodded, and Fiona's heart broke. She hated to think of Spryly leaving, so she could only imagine how difficult it must be for Caleb. In any event, he wasn't in a condition to continue their evening. She stepped back.

"I should leave you to watch over him." Caleb frowned but he didn't disagree. "Thank you for the lovely evening. Dinner was wonderful, and I can't wait to hear the children sing in the lecture room next week."

The corners of Caleb's mouth lifted a fraction. "Me either. But don't leave just yet. I have something for thee." He darted out of the parlor and returned a moment later with a small, rectangular package wrapped in brown paper. He handed it to her.

"Shall I open it now?" she asked, eager to see what book he'd chosen for her. He nodded, so she tore into the paper and discovered not a book at all but a block of... "Chocolate?"

Caleb grinned. "I remembered how much thee enjoyed the drinking chocolate we had at the café, and I thought thee might like to be able to prepare some at home."

His thoughtfulness almost overwhelmed her. No one had ever given her chocolate before. Books, certainly. Lace handkerchiefs, occasionally. But chocolate? She rewrapped the bar in the brown paper and clutched it to her bosom.

"I love it. And I'll think of you with every sip."

"Then when this is all gone, I shall buy thee more." He leaned in and pressed a gentle kiss to her lips.

Chapter Fourteen

Regina had to hold Spryly still while Caleb
unwound the extra blankets and scarves he'd wrapped
around the boy before their journey to the Castle. He and
the rest of the children had walked over from
Georgetown, but Regina and Spryly had followed in a
cab. Spryly hadn't had any more full-on coughing fits
since last week, but Caleb wasn't taking any chances
sending the boy out in the cold air, especially this close
to the canal.

"Aw, leave me wrapped up, Caleb, please," Spryly
begged. "I wanna pretend to be one of the mummies!"

Caleb nearly choked holding back his laughter. It
wouldn't do to let Spryly know just how funny he found
the thought of the boy jumping out at guests in the
exhibition hall.

"Perhaps another time. Thee has a rehearsal to get to
upstairs."

Spryly heaved a sigh that ended in a wheeze, took
Regina's hand, and trudged toward the staircase in the
South Tower. Caleb's arms twitched, wanting to pick
Spryly up and carry him to the lecture room, but he didn't
want to embarrass the boy any more than he already had
by making him ride in a cab while the rest of the kids
walked. He watched Spryly's curly hair bounce as he
made his way slowly up the stairs and closed his eyes for
a moment against a violent rush of emotion that swept

through him.

"Hold on, Spryly," he whispered. "Please hold on."

"Caleb!"

Caleb jumped so hard he tripped over his own feet when he landed and nearly fell over. A strong hand grabbed his bicep and steadied him.

"Sorry about that," Jacob's familiar voice said. "Didn't mean to startle you. I was just so pleased I caught you here."

Heart still pounding from the surprise, Caleb looked up into the face of his best friend. "What is thee doing here?" Jacob detested coming into the city. The canal was bad enough, but it was the ghosts of the old slave auction sites that deeply haunted the physician. Slave trading had been banned in Washington City by the time Caleb arrived, but even nine years after the ban, odd clearings amidst buildings and the occasional crumbling wooden platform stood as somber reminders of that despicable practice.

"Martha told Lyddie you'd be here this afternoon." Jacob gestured to his daughter, who hovered behind him.

Caleb furrowed his brow. "That doesn't answer my question."

Jacob chuckled. "I suppose not." He told Lyddie to go on upstairs to the lecture room and then whipped an envelope out of his pocket and waved it in front of Caleb's face. "I got a reply from Will."

Caleb ripped the envelope from Jacob's fingers. It was already open, and he dug out the letter inside.

Lucky Star Ranch
Placerville, Calif.
November 20, 1859
Dear Jacob,

I am grateful to hear you and Lydia are well and encourage you to make a visit out to California soon to see the ranch. Elizabeth, the boys, and I would all love to see you.

In the meantime, your work with the orphans in Washington makes me proud. I may have gotten the brains in the family, but you certainly inherited the heart. While we are sadly unable to save every child, Elizabeth and I would be pleased to take in this young man you speak of. We've been praying for another child for many years, and it seems God has seen fit to grant us our wish, albeit in a way we did not expect.

I have enclosed fifty dollars. That should be enough to arrange for the boy's travel and that of a chaperone, if needed. I expect you will wait until after the new year to send him, so please reply as soon as you have made the travel arrangements so we know when and where to meet him.

Please tell him that his new family is eager for him to arrive. His older brothers are already looking for just the right pony, and his Mama is making a quilt for his bed.

Keep a weather eye on the situation there in the East, Jacob. The reports we receive of the tensions between the North and South are unsettling, to say the least. You always have a home you and Lydia can come to here in Placerville.

God keep you both.

Your brother,

William

P.S. Is the boy's name really "Spryly"?

Caleb's heart grew heavy as he read the letter. This was it. Spryly would be leaving in only three weeks. He knew the boy would leave one way or the other, and this was certainly the preferable way, but now that he held Will's letter in his hand, the reality of the pending loss hit him. He should be happy. Spryly, unlike so many of the children, had found a family. The best possible family, too, in a place where he would stay healthy and grow strong, just as he deserved to do. Like Ruth never had the chance to do.

But that meant saying goodbye to the boy he had come to love as his own son. Caleb knew when he'd taken this job that he must love the children but not grow too attached. His job was to care for them only until they were placed either with a family or an employer. He had to love them and then let them go.

But he didn't want to.

He gripped the letter so tightly the paper crinkled, and Jacob's solid hand landed on his shoulder.

"I'll miss him too," Jacob said. "But we both know this is the best thing for Spryly."

Caleb nodded and cleared his throat. "'Tis. And I thank thee for arranging it." He drew in and blew out a deep breath as he tucked the letter back into its envelope. "I suppose I shall tell the Meeting tomorrow that I will be traveling to California next month. They'll need to find someone to stand in for me at the home while I'm away."

"Give me a few days to work on that," Jacob said. "I've still got connections with my family's old merchant business up in Boston. I might be able to arrange for him to travel with someone who's headed that way anyhow."

"Again, I thank thee," Caleb said, ashamed at how difficult it was for him to muster any gratitude just then. Jacob and his brother were saving Spryly's life. He searched for something more meaningful to say to his friend.

"Come on." Jacob grabbed his elbow, saving him from having to make any further reply at all. "Let's go upstairs and listen to those kids sing. Lyddie tells me they're breathtaking. Besides," he chuckled, "I expect your lady friend is up there too."

****

By the time Caleb and Jacob made their way to the back of the lecture room, the children were already running through their songs, with Martha accompanying them on the piano. They were halfway through "Hark the Herald Angels Sing," their voices blending in perfect harmony and resonating through the hall.

They were, themselves, the angels, Caleb thought. Then he shifted his gaze slightly to the left and laid eyes on another angel.

Fiona stood a few yards away, listening to the children sing. She didn't seem to have noticed him, and he studied her for a moment, letting his mind wander back to their truncated evening together last week. The way she'd settled so easily onto his lap, and the hungry way she kissed him. His hand drifted to his lips, remembering the pressure of her mouth on his. Then she turned and smiled with a joy that reached her eyes and lit her entire face. He smiled back, fighting the urge to stride over there and kiss her again.

He felt a nudge in his ribcage and turned his gaze back the other direction to see Jacob grinning at him.

"Think I'll go listen with Regina and Lyddie," he whispered, waving one hand toward the front of the hall and giving Caleb a cheeky wink before he walked away.

Caleb sidled up to Fiona as soon as Jacob headed

down the aisle toward the stage where Regina sat in the front row. He laced his fingers through hers and squeezed her hand. She glanced around as if checking to be sure no one was watching, then brushed a quick peck to his cheek. They stood together, hand in hand, and listened to the children finish the song and then move on to "God Rest Ye Merry, Gentlemen."

They'd sounded incredible in the parlor last week, but here in the lecture room's acoustics and with the piano accompanying them, their voices were positively heavenly. The songs themselves were beautiful too. He especially liked the bouncing rhythms of "Good King Wenceslas" and "I Saw Three Ships." Between these songs and books like *A Christmas Carol*, he could understand why more and more people enjoyed celebrating Christmas every year.

He clutched Fiona's hand while the children ran through their songs, unwilling to ever let her go. Though he was losing Spryly, perhaps he might have children of his own someday. Little ones who would bring him the joy of fatherhood without the pain of having to say goodbye. He flicked his gaze to Fiona, and when she caught his eye and smiled, he felt hope that this was more than wishful thinking.

When the children finished rehearsing all the songs once through, Martha called for a short break, and Regina announced that she'd brought along some sugar cookies. The children—and Jacob—sent up a cheer so loud that Martha chastised them to save their voices.

"Would thee like a cookie?" Caleb asked Fiona. "I'm certain Regina brought more than enough."

Fiona laughed. "No, thank you." Still holding his hand, she led him to the last row and settled onto the plush cushion of one of the seats, gesturing to Caleb to do the same. Once he sat, she took his hand again, and his heart soared.

"How is Spryly?" she asked, tilting her head toward the stage a few dozen rows of seats away. "I've been thinking about him."

"Well enough," Caleb said. "He's managed to avoid falling truly ill again. And we received word from Jacob's brother." He pulled the letter out of his coat pocket and handed it to her. She read it, her eyes widening as she scanned down the page. When she reached the bottom, she looked up, beaming.

"Why, Caleb, this is wonderful news." As she continued to stare at him, the joy in her expression slowly faded. "Isn't it?" Before he could manage a reply, she reached out and took his hand. "But of course you're sad he's leaving." She looked up toward the front of the hall where Spryly was swiping another cookie from the tin while Regina was distracted talking to Jacob. "He's quite a special boy."

"That he is," Caleb said. He didn't want to dwell on Spryly's departure any longer. The situation was sad enough on its own, and Fiona's preternatural understanding of his feelings on the topic was going to undo him. He needed to change the subject. "How was Nicole's wedding last week?" he asked. Fiona had seemed apprehensive about the wedding when he first met her, but over time she'd seemed to grow excited about the event. He held his breath, hoping for a positive response.

Fiona's face lit up, and he exhaled. "Beautiful," she said, only a hair's breadth from gushing. "She was such a lovely bride, and she and David seem so happy together." Caleb smiled at the wistful look that crossed her face. If he was going to broach this topic, he wouldn't get a better opportunity.

"I am glad to hear that. I had received the impression that thee was unhappy about the marriage."

Fiona's mouth twisted to one side. He'd noticed she often did that when she was thinking hard, and it made him burn with the urge to kiss her. But he bit his lower lip instead. Secretary Clark could walk into the lecture room at any time, not to mention any of the children could turn a head and spot them.

"I was," Fiona said at last, still gazing out over the sprawling auditorium. "But it was never anything against David. I simply…" She sighed. "It wasn't easy taking over the library after my brother passed. Secretary Clark was the only person who seemed to think a woman was up to the task. And even then he wouldn't have hired just any woman. I got the job because I was already working here and knew the library inside and out."

She turned her eyes back to Caleb. "I don't blame the secretary. He's a good man. This is just how the world is. But when he allowed me to bring Nicole on as my assistant, I'd hoped she and I would usher in a new era where women were valued for more than just cooking and childbearing. So it was disappointing, to say the least, when she announced her engagement and was told she would have to resign her position." She looked down at her hands. "But seeing her on Saturday—well, Seventh Day—" she smiled into her lap, "I don't think she felt like she was giving anything up at all. For her, she's gaining so much."

A flicker of hope sparked in Caleb's chest, but he knew he'd need to choose his next words carefully. "And how about thee?" he said softly. "How does thee feel about marriage?"

The corner of her mouth twisted up again, this time in a coy smile. "Well," she said, dragging out the word, "I suppose that would depend on the man who asked me."

The flicker of hope ignited.

Chapter Fifteen

Fiona arrived at work the following Friday with a lightness to her step. The children's rehearsal in the lecture room last week had gone better than she could ever have dreamed. Secretary Clark had come upstairs and heard the last two or three songs the children rehearsed after they'd had their cookies, and by the end of "Stille Nacht," he was dabbing at his eyes with his handkerchief.

"Marvelous, Mr. Fox, simply marvelous," he said to Caleb, who was still seated next to Fiona. "And precisely what this town—nay, this entire *country*—needs right now. The dulcet voices of these children raised in song celebrating the birth of the Messiah will be a badly needed balm for the frayed nerves of our politicians and our citizenry."

Out of the corner of her eye, Fiona saw Caleb's chest inflate at the secretary's praise, and she almost giggled. Caleb Fox was many things, but a proud man was not one of them. Only a compliment on his children could make him puff up like a rooster. And almost as quickly as he'd expanded, he shrank back to his usual size, and Fiona bit back another giggle, knowing that he must have suddenly remembered himself. She hoped he wasn't too horrified that he'd let pride get the better of him, albeit briefly.

"I thank thee. The children and I sincerely hope their

small offering will bring a sense of peace to all who hear them."

Secretary Clark rubbed his hands together and said he was sending a messenger to the print shop right away to order handbills to post around the city, announcing the concert.

Now, six days later, Fiona was still floating on the joy of the encounter as if she had seen the herald angels with her own eyes. She'd already overheard some talk around town regarding the children's concert, but she knew that Nicole's wedding was contributing to her ebullient mood as well. The ceremony had been beautiful. It was a small affair with only as many guests as could fit in the parlor of Nicole's parents' home, and Fiona had felt honored to be included. Nicole had purchased a new green-silk gown with a fashionably wide skirt, and as she and David exchanged their vows, her face had glowed with a bliss such as Fiona had never seen on her—not even when they would get new books at the library.

So perhaps marriage wasn't as tragic as she'd feared. She supposed there were certainly harder ways to go through life than side by side with a man you loved. And she loved Caleb. She could imagine herself by his side, helping him care for the children, at least in the evenings. Because she was beginning to believe she might not *have* to resign her position at the Smithsonian. She'd been mulling it over ever since her conversation in the lecture room with Caleb last week. True, she had been the convenient choice to take over leadership of the library after George died, but Secretary Clark had been under no obligation to opt for the convenient choice. He would have been well within both tradition and his rights as secretary to find a man for the job.

But he hadn't.

He had turned the library over to Fiona with nary a hesitation. He wouldn't have done that if he didn't think highly of her capabilities, and with the good graces she was earning by having arranged this concert, he might forgive her sex a second time. It wouldn't be the strangest thing to ever happen in Washington City.

More certain was the fact that Caleb was considering proposing. There couldn't be any other explanation for his question regarding her feelings on marriage. He'd need to speak with Michael first. With her father and only brother both dead, her brother-in-law would be the man Caleb would need to ask for her hand. Michael would be stunned, and Fiona laughed, thinking of her kind but ever-so-proper brother-in-law going slack-jawed.

"What's got you so happy this morning?" Martha asked, snapping Fiona out of her reverie. Fiona hadn't even heard the girl come in, and she turned and gave Martha a wide smile.

"I simply cannot wait for the concert next week," she said. Martha narrowed her eyes, clearly disbelieving this story, and Fiona hurried to give her a list of small jobs to complete around the library.

By the afternoon, the temperature began to drop, and it didn't take long for the cavernous library to turn chilly. Fiona warmed her hands by the stove in one corner, dreaming of the steaming cup of drinking chocolate she planned to make for herself tonight after supper.

The block of chocolate had been such a thoughtful gift. She only wished she'd been able to stay at the home longer that evening to make herself and Caleb each a cup to enjoy together. She'd have to go back some evening soon, perhaps even on Christmas Day. That could be a good bit of fun, now that she thought about it. She could take over some gingerbread as well. It made for quite the cozy picture, curled up next to Caleb on the settee, both of them with cups of chocolate, a plate of gingerbread on the table in front of them, the children asleep upstairs...

"Miss?" A man's voice shattered her daydream. "Could you help me find some information on the fall of the Roman Empire?"

The fall of the Roman Empire was only the beginning. As soon as she'd directed the man to Edward Gibbons's six-volume treatise on the subject, another man popped in asking for a street map of Pittsburgh. When she told him the library didn't have one, he asked for Boston instead. No sooner had she found him the map than yet another fellow arrived and said, "I'm looking for a book. I've forgotten the title, I'm afraid, but it was blue." And so it went. Once or twice she turned to pass a patron along to Martha, only to see the girl was bouncing between requests as frantically as she was.

While pulling down an old guidebook meant for travelers along the Oregon Trail, Fiona spotted Secretary Clark entering the library. She quickly gave the guidebook to the patron who'd requested it and started to cross the room to her boss. But she'd taken no more than five steps before another patron stepped into her path, asking for help with some research about Thomas Jefferson. Over the man's shoulder, she saw Martha scurry up to the secretary, and she relaxed a degree. Hopefully Martha could take a message.

Fiona turned back to the man inquiring about Jefferson, but she kept glancing over her shoulder at

Martha and Secretary Clark. Martha waved one arm around as if to indicate a bank of shelves, but the secretary shook his head. Martha shifted her weight from one foot to the other and back again, then looked over her own shoulder at Fiona. Their eyes locked, and Fiona knew her apprentice needed help. Secretary Clark seemed to be in an unusually impatient mood, and Martha's expression looked panicked.

"My apologies," Fiona told her patron, "but I must see to the Smithsonian Secretary. I'll return directly." The man frowned, and Fiona scurried away before he could reply.

"Miss Ellicott, thank goodness," Secretary Clark said. "I need the donation records from 1857. I have a widow up in arms over an item her late husband donated that she claims was only a loan. I need to pull the deed of gift before her attorney sends a mob after me."

"I'm so sorry, Miss Ellicott," Martha said, addressing Fiona in the formal manner she used in front of patrons and other Smithsonian staff. "I've not accessed those records before, and I don't know where they are."

"It's all right, my dear," the secretary said before Fiona could respond. "I know you've not been here long." He patted Martha's head and fixed his gaze on Fiona. "Now, if you would, please, Miss Ellicott. The matter really is quite urgent."

"Of course, sir, right this way." Fiona beckoned for him to follow and took off between two rows of shelves toward the back of the library where the records were kept. "Was it the first half of the year or the second?"

"The first, I believe."

Fiona pulled down the appropriate gift record book

and handed it to him. Secretary Clark laid it on a nearby table and started flipping the pages with careless speed. Fiona cringed, praying none of the pages would tear. She wasn't nearly as skilled at book repair as George had been.

"Aha!" the secretary said at last, stabbing a page with one finger. "Deed of gift, *not* a loan agreement." He slammed the book shut and shoved it under one arm, and Fiona winced again. "I'll be very happy to show this to Widow Hawkins's attorney." He studied Fiona for a moment, and she could almost hear gears whirring in his brain. "After the first of the year, I'm going to take out an advertisement for another library assistant. I'm certain your young apprentice will be a great asset once she's all trained up, but even with her, I gather you could use more help."

Fiona blinked a few times, surprised by his offer. The Castle itself had been so expensive to build that she'd always been reluctant to ask for resources.

"I appreciate your frugality, Miss Ellicott," Secretary Clark said, startling Fiona again. Could the man read her mind? "But there's no denying the library is growing, both in the size of its collection and its popularity among the citizenry. You will need more help."

The smile he leveled on her glowed with such pride that Fiona felt hot tears prick the corners of her eyes. She'd never known a father's pride—she'd been only three years old when Papa died—but in this moment, she knew she had an idea of what it must be like.

"Thank you, sir," she said. "Martha is a great help, but we certainly could use a third employee. I must admit I *was* already feeling shorthanded before Miss Daly left."

Secretary Clark huffed. "Yes, Miss Daly. A wonderful assistant. A shame she had to run off and get married. We just lost a woman in the Laboratory of Natural History to marriage also. She tried to convince me to let her return after the wedding. Can you believe it? As if the Board of Regents would ever allow that." He shook his head. "I'm glad I needn't worry about *you* losing your head. You've got more sense than to throw away everything you've worked for. Anyway," he said, his expression brightening, "thank you for this. We'll meet after the new year and discuss that job advertisement."

He turned and strode away, leaving Fiona gulping for air like she'd just been punched in the gut.

Chapter Sixteen

The next day, Caleb climbed the steps to Fiona's front door, his stomach swirling with nerves.

This is merely a dinner out, he told himself, *like we've done before.*

The frightening part would come later while they strolled along the Mall. The south side of the Mall, of course, farthest from the canal. The route would also take them right behind the Castle—the perfect spot, Caleb felt, for him to ask Fiona the question he wanted to ask.

His Meeting had agreed on First Day that he and Fiona were a good match. Of course, they'd prefer if Fiona became a member of the Meeting herself, but they were content with her attending regularly. And for her part, Fiona seemed happy to attend. She'd already asked if he'd come for her again tomorrow, which he'd readily agreed to do. He couldn't wait for her to help him share the good news with both the Meeting and the children tomorrow morning.

He hesitated before he knocked on the door. Perhaps he should have spoken with Fiona's brother-in-law first. Michael seemed a reasonable fellow, and Caleb felt confident he would agree, but the idea of having to ask another man's permission to propose to a woman had always made his lip curl. Getting discernment from the Meeting to ensure the way forward was clear and wise was one thing, but asking Michael's permission as if he *owned* Fiona... Caleb couldn't reconcile with the idea. Besides, Fiona oversaw the entire Smithsonian Library. The woman could make her own decisions, for goodness' sake. He raised his fist and rapped sharply on the door.

Susan opened the door and welcomed him inside. She left him alone in the parlor while she fetched Fiona, and he shifted nervously, unable to sit. Goodness, this must be what it felt like to be Spryly. He chuckled.

After only a moment or two, Fiona entered the parlor. Immediately, Caleb knew something was off. She clutched one hand so tightly in the other her knuckles were white, and though she smiled at him, the joy didn't reach her eyes.

Bless her, she was nervous too. He stifled another chuckle. After their discussion last week during the children's rehearsal, she must have worked out what he was up to. He was a little disappointed he wouldn't surprise her, but perhaps it was better not to catch the lady off guard. He stepped forward and reached for her hands. Her fingers were cold.

"You look lovely, as always," he said.

She smiled tightly again. "Thank you."

Goodness, she really *was* nervous. His best chance of setting her at ease likely was to act as though everything were normal. The two of them were simply headed out for a nice dinner and a stroll. He offered her his arm.

"Shall we?"

****

Fiona was oddly quiet throughout their dinner at the café where they'd first discussed the children's Christmas concert. Caleb could hardly believe that was

142

less than two months ago. Since then, Jacob had arranged for Spryly to go to California, Martha had started an apprenticeship at the Smithsonian, and he himself was hoping to wed—something he'd given up on long ago. Not to mention he was also enjoying Christmas carols for the first time. He shook his head. How quickly life could change.

Fiona perked up some when he ordered drinking chocolate for both of them after the meal, but he couldn't shake the feeling that something was wrong. Something deeper than nerves. It wasn't like Fiona not to be forthcoming with him, but she'd met every gentle query into her wellbeing with a dismissive wave of her hand. She must be tired. But for Martha, who was still learning, Fiona was on her own at the library now that Nicole had left. He imagined it must be a good deal of work. He'd witnessed some of the patrons there being needier than his children.

The weather had turned brisk in recent days—they were likely to have their first hard freeze of the winter any day now—but Caleb couldn't imagine a better setting for his proposal than outside the Castle. So when they finished their meal, he helped Fiona into her coat, and they set off for the Mall.

Caleb almost immediately wished he hadn't eaten so much at dinner, but the roast mutton and potatoes had been so good it had broken through his earlier bout of nerves, and he'd polished off his entire helping. Now, with Fiona on his arm on their way to his chosen destination, the meal churned in his stomach. Surely it was excitement, not anxiety.

As they strolled along the south side of the Mall, the wind, thankfully, blowing north, drawing away the canal's stench, Caleb reflected briefly how if the city would fill in the canal, the Mall could be a pleasant park. The scraggly trees near the Castle would eventually fill in, and perhaps the Smithsonian could expand and build a few more museums for visitors to enjoy. Wouldn't hurt to finish building the monument to George Washington, either. Construction of the obelisk had been halted since he moved to town, and its prospects didn't look too promising. A shame, really. With clean air and a completed monument, this town could look quite lovely. He smiled. Washington City was a lot like Spryly: a rough exterior but with unlimited potential if only it were tapped.

When they reached the Castle, Caleb stopped and turned to Fiona, taking both her hands in his.

This was it.

He drew in a deep breath to steady himself, hoping against hope that he wouldn't butcher the little speech Jacob had helped him compose. Fiona's eyes glittered in the yellow light thrown off by the nearby streetlamp. He let himself bask in the sight for a moment, hardly able to believe that he'd get to look into these beautiful eyes every day for the rest of his life.

"Fiona," he began, relieved that his voice wasn't shaking too badly, "before I met thee, I'd grown quite used to being alone. I had the children, of course, but I had concluded that a wife and children of my own were not to be. Then one day, I came here to find some information about President Washington, and I found so much more. Dropping my handkerchief that day was the best thing I've ever done."

Tears welled in Fiona's eyes, and Caleb felt the hot sting in his own.

"Caleb, I—"

Caleb laid one gloved finger over Fiona's lips. If he stopped now, he wasn't sure he could work up the courage to get going again.

"Fiona, I love thee." The words fell from his lips so easily, as if they'd been longing to be spoken, and though he'd always striven to speak plainly and honestly, he knew he'd never said anything truer. "I love thee, and I want to spend the rest of my days with thee. I haven't much to offer, but I can assure thee that thee would never want for love and affection." He reached up and rested his gloved hand on her cheek. "Would thee do me the great honor of marrying me?"

Fiona's gaze flicked toward the Castle looming next to them, a towering, Gothic watchman rising out of the dark winter sky. She was silent for so long she might have been holding her own personal Meeting for Worship. Finally, she closed her eyes, and a single tear cut a rivulet down her cheek. Caleb's stomach fell with it.

"I'm so sorry," she said, her voice husky and barely louder than a whisper. She opened her eyes but dropped her gaze to her feet. "I can't."

Caleb's stomach bottomed out, and he dropped his hand from her cheek. This wasn't right. This *couldn't* be right. Fiona was supposed to say yes and fall into his arms. She was supposed to accept his proposal here outside the Castle, and then they'd live happily ever after like in the fairy tales little Patricia loved so much. Fiona couldn't have said no. He must have misheard.

"Fiona, what..." His chest heaved. It felt like someone was cinching a rope around him, cutting off his breath. He fought to draw air. "Doesn't...doesn't thee love me back?" He wasn't sure he could bear to hear her answer, but he had to know. "I thought that—"

"It isn't that," Fiona said, the rest of her tears breaking free and cascading down her perfect cheeks. "I simply can't marry you. You don't know what you're asking. I just...I can't see you any longer. I shouldn't even have come out tonight. I'm sorry. I'm so sorry." Casting one last, quick glance up at the Castle, she turned and fled, her skirts flying behind her.

"Wait!" Caleb called. He raced after her, catching her after only a few steps. He gripped her arm but almost immediately let her go. He wouldn't keep her here against her will, no matter how painful it was to watch her leave. "Please," he said, fighting to keep any semblance of composure, "please, at least let me get thee a cab." He couldn't let her walk home alone in the dark. It wasn't safe. Fiona nodded and walked next to him, though not holding his arm, to the nearest street corner, where Caleb flagged down a hansom cab.

Fiona let him help her into the cab. He racked his brain, trying to find the words that could change her mind, make everything right, but language deserted him. Something had failed between them, that much was certain. But what? Barely a week ago they'd been teasing each other with talk of marriage. Now, he closed the cab door behind her. Tearfully, she held his gaze through the window until the driver clucked to his horse, and the cab lurched away.

As soon as the cab disappeared around a corner toward Capitol Hill, Caleb finally let his tears fall.

"I shall hold thee in the Light," he choked out to the empty street.

****

Caleb awoke the next morning to a pounding in his head and an even more insistent pounding on his bedroom door. He groaned and rolled over. He'd never imbibed in drink, yet he knew this must be what those hangovers Jacob had told him about felt like. He blinked and rubbed the grit from his eyes, wondering why his nightshirt felt so crinkly. Then he looked down and realized he was fully dressed.

Last night flooded back. His proposal, Fiona's refusal. Worse, her saying she couldn't see him anymore. Her utter lack of an explanation. She owed him nothing, he knew that. But an explanation would have been kind.

After she left in the cab, he'd sat on the cold ground outside the Castle and stared up at the building for a long time, trying to discern how everything had fallen to pieces. It wasn't until one of Washington's few policemen had come by and snapped at him that there was no loitering on Smithsonian grounds that he'd finally started the long walk home to Georgetown.

Other than the clock in the parlor striking two, the house was silent when he arrived, and he'd trudged up the stairs to his bedroom, where he'd fallen onto his bed fully clothed and fallen into a deep, dreamless sleep.

Now, all he wanted to do was roll over and close his eyes again, try to sleep off this throbbing in his skull, but the pounding on the door wouldn't stop. With another groan, he hauled himself to his feet and stumbled across the room.

"Merciful heavens," Regina said when Caleb opened the door, "thee gave me a fright. It's unlike thee to oversleep. Meeting is in twenty minutes."

Meeting. Of course. Today was First Day. The day he was supposed to escort Fiona into Meeting as his fiancée and announce the happy news to everyone.

"Yes, Meeting," he mumbled. "Of course. I'll be down straightaway." He started to close the door, but Regina shoved through and stepped into his bedroom and right up into his face. She narrowed her eyes and studied him.

"Thee most certainly will not. Thee will go straight back to bed. I will tell the children thee isn't well, and I'll bring up a bowl of broth when we return. Now, into bed." She glanced him over once more. "But put thy nightclothes on first."

Caleb didn't enjoy being ordered around like a child, but he was so relieved to avoid Meeting this morning and even more relieved to be able to return to bed that he didn't complain. He shucked off his rumpled clothes from last night and pulled a nightshirt over his head. As he picked up his trousers and tossed them on the tumbledown armchair in the corner, a white square of cloth fluttered out of one pocket.

Ruth's handkerchief. The item that had begun this entire ordeal. Now it was all he had to remind himself of both Ruth *and* Fiona. Swallowing back a sob, he plucked it off the floor and folded it carefully into a perfect square with his embroidered initials facing out. He placed it on his night table and crawled into bed.

****

The next thing Caleb knew, Jacob was looming over him.

"Oh, Caleb, I'm so sorry," Jacob said. He slung an arm around Caleb's shoulders and heaved him up so they sat side by side on the edge of the bed, Caleb's head still spinning from being jolted out of sleep.

"Did Regina send for thee?" he mumbled.

Jacob nodded. "Sent Eric to fetch me. Said you looked a fright this morning and missed Meeting. I guessed what must have happened." Jacob was the only person Caleb had told about his plans to propose, and now Caleb was glad that he'd told his best friend but no one else.

"Does she know?"

"Not unless you told her. I haven't breathed a word to anyone, not even Lyddie, that you were proposing." He paused. "I cannot believe she declined. From what you told me, things seemed so certain."

"They were." Caleb scrubbed his hands through his hair. "At least I thought so."

"What happened?"

Caleb sighed. He didn't want to recount last night, but a small part of him hoped that Jacob might have a solution. He told his friend everything that happened from the time he picked Fiona up at her house until he put her in the cab at the end of the evening. Jacob listened quietly, periodically patting Caleb's shoulder.

"She didn't say why?" Jacob said when Caleb finished his tale.

Caleb shook his head. "She implied she loved me but she couldn't see me any longer. And she certainly couldn't marry me. She said I didn't know what I was asking."

"I'm so sorry, Caleb," Jacob said again. "It's strange she didn't give you a reason."

"I don't know how I'm going to face her at the concert on Seventh Day." Caleb rubbed his face with both palms. "Maybe I can hide in the back of the hall."

"Listen, we'll worry about Saturday when we get to Saturday," Jacob said. "Right now, let's get you dressed and put some food in you."

Caleb hauled himself to his feet and headed for his wardrobe for a clean shirt and trousers. Halfway there, he heard a small sneeze, and he looked over his shoulder at Jacob, who shrugged.

"Not me," he said. They both glanced at the closed door. Jacob rose and went to open it. Martha stood on the other side, holding a tray. Wisps of steam curled up from the bowl on the tray, and a small dish of soda crackers sat next to it. Martha blushed.

"Regina asked me to bring this up." She shifted her gaze to Caleb. "Oh, you're up!" Relief washed across her face. "Are you well?"

"Quite," Caleb said. "Just overtired. I thank thee for the tray. Please pass my thanks along to Regina as well."

Martha gave him a strange look but nodded and scurried out of the room. Jacob closed the door and pointed to the tray.

"Get dressed, and then I want you to eat everything here. I know from experience that it won't heal the heartache, but it'll give you the strength you need to care for the children who are still depending on you."

The children who, once the concert was over, would ask why Fiona no longer came to visit them. Caleb hadn't thought it possible, but he felt his heart break just a little bit more.

Chapter Seventeen

Fiona arrived at work Monday morning still in a daze. She'd turned down Caleb's offer of marriage. The first man she'd fallen in love with, and who confessed to loving her, and she'd turned him down. She still couldn't conceive that it had really happened, and she couldn't shake the last image she had of him, closing the door to the cab, his handsome face wrenched in sorrow.

When the cab dropped her off at home Saturday night, she'd fled to her bedroom and wouldn't emerge, despite Susan's pleas that she tell her what had happened. Only when Michael threatened to race to Georgetown and pummel Caleb for whatever it was that he'd done to her did she finally come out. Even then, she refused to tell them the whole story, only that she had broken things off with Caleb, but he'd done nothing ungentlemanly. Michael simmered down after that, but Susan gave her a long, sympathetic look, and Fiona guessed that her sister knew exactly what had transpired.

She'd hoped that coming to work this morning would make her feel better, would validate her decision somehow, but she only felt worse. This library she'd always loved so much felt cold and foreign, and she suddenly remembered her mother's stories of arriving in America from England when Fiona was a baby. Even though they spoke English and looked like everyone else in their new neighborhood in New York City, they were still different. This place that should have been familiar and comfortable still reminded them that they didn't quite belong. As a child, Fiona had brushed off those stories. She'd been only three months old when the family arrived in America, so to her, America was home, the place where she belonged. She'd never understood how her mother had felt during those early years—until this morning.

But she'd *had* to come to work today, and she had to keep coming to work every day until she was too old and infirm to continue. Her dear departed brother had worked so hard to establish this library, and he'd entrusted it to her care. And what of Susan's hard work? Laboring away so Fiona and George could stay in school and eventually learn librarianship. If Fiona allowed herself to lose her head over a man, she wouldn't merely be giving up her career, she'd be disregarding the sacrifices her family had made to get her this career.

Her chest ached like she had an entire set of encyclopedias sitting on it. Why couldn't she have met Caleb a few years earlier? Two and a half years would have done it, before George died and she took charge of the library. When she was still merely George's assistant, she could have seen herself stepping away from her career if she found love. But now? She swallowed hard. She couldn't. She was in too rare and enviable a position.

If only she hadn't had to break two hearts to keep it.

She tried to distract herself with recording some new books in the catalog but then realized she should probably save that for when Martha arrived. It would be a good skill to teach the girl, and she needed to teach her as much as possible before Secretary Clark hired the new assistant, whom Fiona would need to train as well. She was hoping Martha would know enough by then to help teach the new employee.

Come to think of it, where *was* Martha? Fiona checked the clock on the desk. Nine thirty. Martha should have arrived an hour ago. Had Caleb prohibited her from coming in? Surely not. He wouldn't deny Martha this opportunity because of his own bruised pride. And if the child were sick, surely he or Regina, or even Dr. Carter, would have sent a message to let her know.

A chill coursed through her. What if something had happened to Martha on the way into town today? As a rule, the cab drivers in Washington City were reliable, but suppose they'd taken a route through one of the slums and been attacked? The ne'er-do-wells didn't typically attack moving vehicles, but it wasn't unheard of. Her heart in her throat, she strode toward the library door. There were no patrons yet. She'd lock up and set off in search of Martha. She'd follow the route the cabs most likely took here from Georgetown, and if she reached the home with no sign of the girl, she'd alert Caleb. Painful as it would be to see him after how she left things Saturday night, she had to think of Martha first.

As soon as she stepped through the library door into the West Range, she spotted not one but two familiar slight figures plodding slowly, hand in hand, toward her. Stifling a cry of relief, Fiona dashed across the room and wrapped Martha and Spryly up in her arms.

"I was so worried," Fiona said into Martha's dark hair. "When you didn't arrive on time, I thought—" Well, better not to say what she'd thought. It would frighten the children. "I was so worried," she repeated.

153

"I apologize." Martha stepped back from Fiona's embrace. "I didn't mean to make you worry. I just…"

"She didn't know what to say," Spryly said, taking a step back as well.

"Whatever do you mean?" Fiona asked.

Martha and Spryly shared a glance, and the little boy waved his hands at Martha in a "go on" gesture. Martha sighed and stared at her shoes.

"I can't work here any longer," she said, her voice trembling.

Fiona's jaw clenched. Caleb was forbidding Martha to continue her apprenticeship after all. She could hardly believe it. She thought she knew him better than that. Perhaps she'd been right to break things off. Oh, she was going to give that man a piece of her mind.

"I will speak with Caleb," she said, unable to keep the sharp edge out of her voice. "I'll not allow him to keep you from this opportunity."

"Caleb ain't stoppin' nothing," Spryly said. "He don't even know."

Fiona furrowed her brow and turned to the boy. "What doesn't he know?"

"That Martha's quittin'."

Fiona cocked her head and studied Martha, the girl's head still down, gaze still on her scuffed shoes. Fiona took the children by the hand and led them to a bench along one wall of the West Range and told them to sit with her.

"All right," she said, when they were all settled, "how about you start at the top and tell me everything?"

Spryly opened his mouth, but Martha held up a hand and silenced him. She drew in a shuddering breath and slowly lifted her gaze to meet Fiona's eyes.

"Caleb doesn't know this, but I overheard him and Jacob talking yesterday. I don't know what happened between you, and it's none of my business anyway, but I know he's heartbroken." She took in another shaky breath. "When my folks died, Caleb rescued me. I could have ended up on the streets or worse, but he gave me a home. You'll never know how much I appreciate everything you've done for me, Fiona, but it feels disloyal to him to keep working here. I'm sorry." Tears filled the girl's dark eyes, and she tore her gaze away from Fiona's.

Fiona's throat tightened. She didn't know what to say and found herself looking to Spryly for help. The curly-haired boy gnawed his lower lip, then nudged Martha.

"You want I should tell her?" he said. Martha nodded, and Spryly sighed and looked back at Fiona. "We can't do the Christmas concert neither."

Fiona gasped like she'd just been doused with cold water. "Whatever do you mean? You've been preparing for weeks. Everyone's so excited."

"Yeah, but we can't do it no more," Spryly said. His chin quivered, and he chomped down hard on his lower lip.

"Whyever not?"

Spryly scratched the back of his head and looked at Martha, who was still staring into her lap. When she didn't notice him, he nudged her in the ribs. "What was the reason again?"

Martha looked up, tears staining her cheeks. "Imagine how Caleb would feel, having to come back here," she said, her voice breaking with emotion. "Not to mention myself, knowing I'll never get to—" She buried her face in her hands and wept softly. Spryly wrapped a skinny arm around her shoulders.

Fiona ached to take both children in her arms again, but she suddenly felt it was no longer her place to do so. She hadn't just chosen her career over Caleb; she'd chosen it over the children too. Rather than making her sad, the realization infuriated her, reminding her once again that only women had to make that choice. Men could have both.

Martha lifted her head and patted Spryly's knee. "We should go. Eric and Elias will be able to cover up your absence only so long."

"Caleb doesn't even know you're here?" Fiona asked. This was nearly as shocking as Martha's resignation and Spryly's announcement that they weren't going to perform the concert. She knew how much Caleb valued truthfulness, and she'd always admired how well he'd instilled it in the children.

"He doesn't *not* know I'm here," Spryly said. "He just doesn't *know* know."

"We're going to tell him everything as soon as we return," Martha said. "Which we should do before he has cause to worry." Still blinking away tears, she stood, prompting Spryly to stand as well. Fiona leapt to her feet too.

"Please," she said, desperate now, "don't leave. We can talk this through. I'll send a message to Caleb so he doesn't worry."

Martha shook her head. "I'm so sorry. Truly, I am." Another flood of tears broke forth from her red-rimmed eyes, and she grabbed Spryly's hand and dragged him away. Spryly stumbled along with her, glancing one last time over his shoulder and giving Fiona a little wave.

Fiona's head spun as she once again struggled to believe that what had just happened was real. She was still trying to collect herself when Secretary Clark strode into the West Range. She tried to duck behind a display case, but she was too slow. The secretary spotted her, his brow creasing with concern, and hustled over. When he reached her, he laid a hand on her shoulder.

"Miss Ellicott? Are you quite well?"

Fiona burst into tears.

****

Immediately after closing the library that afternoon, Fiona raced back to Capitol Hill, still burning with embarrassment over sobbing in front of her employer. For his part, Secretary Clark had handled it well—he had three daughters, after all—but he'd been none too pleased when Fiona had to tell him that Saturday's concert was canceled.

"Canceled?" he said, his thick, gray eyebrows shooting up nearly to his hairline. "Whatever for?"

After the secretary's outburst last week about women losing their heads over men, Fiona didn't dare tell him the true reason, but she couldn't bear to lie either.

"Stage fright." It was nearly true, if one considered that the children were afraid that their performing on the Smithsonian stage would be too painful for Caleb.

Secretary Clark's eyebrows dropped to their usual latitude, and he narrowed his eyes, clearly not believing her.

"Miss Ellicott, I have had dozens of handbills posted and distributed all over town. Dozens more people, including many powerful politicians, have personally congratulated me on this idea and have told me how much they look forward to the children's performance."

Fiona shrank back a few steps in shame as the secretary continued.

"I needn't remind you of the tension we've all been living under this year. With the John Brown affair over, people are now beginning to squabble over next year's presidential election. Already! With eleven months to go." He shook his head. "You *must* find a way to get the children to perform. So many of the citizens of Washington City are counting on this concert to help them forget their worries and lift their spirits for this most sacred of holidays."

The scholar in her wanted to argue that Easter was more sacred even than Christmas, but Fiona didn't see what good it would do right then. Besides, the most pertinent point would remain: Not only had Fiona broken the heart of the man she loved along with those of a dozen orphans, but she was about to disappoint the entire city as well.

"Well done, Fiona," she muttered as she strode briskly along the sidewalks toward home. "You've ruined Christmas for seventy-five thousand people."

She had to sort this out, but how? No matter which way she looked at it, she had to choose between the Castle and Caleb and the children, and both options left her brokenhearted. She needed to talk it through with someone, but she wasn't sure her sister would understand. Susan had never had to choose between her family and her life's work. For Susan, they were one and the same. Indeed, how many women *at all* had ever had to make that choice? Fiona was the first woman ever employed at the Smithsonian.

She screeched to a halt near the Capitol Building, where workers clanged away, high in the sky, building the new iron dome.

She'd been the first woman employed at the Smithsonian, but not the last. And the woman hired after her *had* faced that decision.

She made a sharp right turn and nearly sprinted toward Nicole's new home.

Nicole answered the door on Fiona's third pounding knock. Fiona was startled to find her friend unaltered since she'd last seen her at her wedding a couple weeks ago. She wasn't sure what she'd expected to have changed, but she hadn't expected Nicole to look so…like herself. Her dark, curly hair was wrestled, as usual, into a chignon, and she wore a blue day dress Fiona had seen on her so many times at the Castle.

"Goodness gracious, Fiona!" Nicole said, her eyes widening. "What's happened? Are you all right?"

Fiona tucked a lock of hair that had come loose in her hurry to get here behind her ear. Her lungs burned from running in the cold air, and she knew her cheeks and nose must be pink. She probably looked a fright.

"I think I've made a terrible mistake."

The panic in Nicole's eyes faded, and she nodded knowingly. "Very likely. Come inside and tell me about it."

Fiona settled onto the settee in the parlor while Nicole went to the kitchen to make some tea. While she waited, Fiona glanced around the room. She'd not been in Nicole and David's new home yet. It was a smaller rowhouse than the one she shared with her family and more modestly furnished, but it was cozy and comfortable with a crackling fireplace in one corner. When she'd entered, she'd spotted a staircase at the end of a hallway and guessed the bedrooms were upstairs.

She smiled, imagining the noise that would eventually emanate from the second floor from the children she knew Nicole and David hoped to have.

It reminded her of the Friends' home, only smaller, and the thought made her chest ache anew. It struck her that she'd likely never see Spryly again. With the concert called off, she'd have no cause to before the boy left for California. She reached into her pocket to grab her handkerchief so she could dab away the tears rising to her eyes, but the handkerchief made her think of Caleb, and she couldn't hold back her sobs.

Nicole rushed into the room, a tea tray rattling precariously in her hands. She set it on a side table and sank onto the settee next to Fiona. She put an arm around Fiona's shoulders and pulled her close.

"Something happened with Caleb, didn't it?"

Fiona nodded and settled her head on Nicole's shoulder, indulging herself in several moments of self-pity before sitting up and wiping the tears from her face. Nicole moved to the side table, fixed two cups of tea, and handed one to Fiona.

"Now," she said, "tell me everything I've missed."

Fiona began with her conversation with Caleb in the lecture room during the children's rehearsal, wept through her rejecting his proposal two nights ago, and concluded with Secretary Clark's not-so-veiled command that she find a way to make the concert on Saturday happen.

"But I don't see how," she wailed. "I can't force the children to sing if they don't want to. And bless them, they've backed out to protect Caleb's feelings." She blew her nose loudly into her handkerchief. "I've ruined Christmas for the entire city!"

Nicole patted her shoulder. "I wouldn't go that far." She paused, and Fiona looked up to see her friend wearing a contemplative expression. She'd seen this face enough to know that Nicole was working out how to say something. "Besides," she said at last, "I think the heart of the problem is that you're miserable because you've pushed Caleb out of your life."

"And hurt a dozen children in the process," Fiona said, sniffling.

"Yes, that as well." Nicole paused again, and this time, she tilted her head and studied Fiona for a moment. "Why *did* you turn him down? The two of you seemed so happy together."

Fiona hesitated. Not wanting to insult Nicole and her choices, she'd glossed over that part of the story. She lowered her gaze and chewed on her lip, trying to craft a response that would be both truthful and inoffensive. In the end, she wasn't sure she could accomplish both, so she simply said, "I didn't want to give up the Smithsonian."

"I understand that completely," Nicole said, nodding. "It was a difficult decision for me as well."

Fiona's head snapped up. She'd no idea Nicole had harbored doubts about leaving her job for marriage. "It was?"

Nicole laughed. "Of course it was! It's the Smithsonian, for goodness' sake. How many women get to work in a library at all, let alone one of the nation's *premiere* libraries?"

That was an awfully generous description, Fiona thought. The libraries she'd known in New York City were much larger, with vastly more comprehensive collections than the Smithsonian's, to say nothing of

Harvard's Gore Hall. But, she supposed, if Congress continued to fund the Institution well, it could one day lead the nation. Either way, Nicole's point was made.

"I never knew you felt that way," she said.

The room echoed with another of Nicole's laughs. "Of course I did. Because I wasn't merely working at the Smithsonian. I was working at the Smithsonian under the direction of another woman. Name another library where *that's* ever happened. I earned a good salary that I could spend however I wished. Believe me, I had to think long and hard about accepting David's proposal."

"How did you decide?"

Nicole shrugged. "I've always wanted a family. Ultimately, I decided that was more important to me than a job."

Fiona growled. "You never should have had to make that choice. Men don't."

"No, they don't, and it isn't fair. But there was nothing I could do about that, and someday, when I'm looking back over my life, I know that this is the path I would have most regretted not taking." Nicole waved a hand, indicating the home she shared with her new husband. "And it isn't as though I'm unable to continue doing important work. I'm helping build the new dome on the Capitol Building."

Now it was Fiona's turn to laugh. "How's that?"

One corner of Nicole's mouth twisted up in a wry smile. "Apart from keeping my husband fed, I've been sending in goodies to the entire construction crew. Last week, I even took a page out of your book and made up an entire vat of drinking chocolate. It was cold that day, too, and it sure did lift the men's spirits."

Fiona stared at Nicole in admiration. She knew

David was one of the craftsmen working on the new dome—she'd probably passed by him on the way here—but she'd never considered the contributions of the men's wives to the project. She suddenly remembered an elderly neighbor she'd known back in New York City when she was just a child. The woman had been a child herself during the Revolutionary War, and she used to entertain Fiona with tales of the home front during the war.

"The men may have been fighting the battles," she'd said once, "but who do you think was back home on the farms, growing the food that kept them fed and able to fight? Who do you think was raising the sheep and spinning the wool to make uniforms and blankets? The women and the slaves, that's who. No, my dear, the army did not win our independence on their own."

"We may not be on the front lines where we belong," Nicole said, as if reading Fiona's thoughts, "but this country couldn't do a thing without us."

Chapter Eighteen

On Sixth Day morning, Caleb was trying without success to get Spryly and Eric to work on their sums. Spryly was unusually melancholy, and Eric kept complaining of a bellyache. Caleb couldn't blame either of them. He'd felt sad and sick, too, ever since Martha and Spryly returned from their sojourn to the Smithsonian the other day and confessed what they'd been up to.

His stomach churned thinking about poor Martha giving up her apprenticeship for him. Had he known she could hear him on First Day, he never would have told Jacob what had happened with Fiona. Martha didn't need to be concerned with it, and she certainly shouldn't have thrown away such an incredible opportunity.

And then the concert. Apparently, after overhearing Caleb's confessions to Jacob, Martha had gathered the children and explained what had happened. Together, they held their own little Meeting for Business and decided that they should not perform on Christmas Eve. In any other situation, Caleb would have burst with pride at their reaching consensus like true Friends, but this crushed him. Nothing he said changed their minds, not even scolding them, asking if he'd taught them nothing about integrity and making good on their commitments. They weren't going back to the Castle, and that was that.

Just as Caleb was about to declare the lesson futile

and give up—none of the other children were doing particularly well on their schoolwork either—Regina appeared in the doorway of the classroom and told him Jacob was downstairs.

If this wasn't the definition of divine providence, he didn't know what was. He told the children to amuse themselves quietly for a few minutes and raced downstairs.

"You've no idea what a merciful rescue this is," he said as he stepped into the parlor. Jacob turned around from where he'd been adjusting the time on the grandfather clock that never seemed to quite keep up with the day. He held his pocket watch up to the clock, compared the two, then tucked his watch back in his pocket.

"Saving lives is my calling." He reached out and shook Caleb's hand. "And I've news about a very special one."

Caleb felt his eyebrows jump. Had Jacob seen Fiona? Had he spoken with her? He gestured to the armchairs near the fireplace, and they both sat, Caleb perching on the edge of his seat and leaning forward toward Jacob.

"Tell me everything."

"I received a wire from a family friend up in Boston," Jacob said. "He's taking the Panama route to California after the first of the year and will be happy to chaperone Spryly on the journey. His ship's leaving from New York City, so you only need to take him that far. Elmer will take care of him from there." He smiled. "You won't have to be gone nearly as long as you'd feared."

"Oh." Caleb sagged back in his chair, feeling foolish. Of course Jacob hadn't spoken to Fiona. Why would he?

"I already looked at the timetables for you." Jacob pulled a piece of folded paper out of his pocket and passed it to Caleb. "One train from here to Philadelphia, where you'll stay overnight, then the next morning catch another train to New York City. You'll be there and back again in less than a week."

Less than a week. It shouldn't be that easy, Caleb thought. It shouldn't be so easy to send someone you loved so far away.

Though if he'd learned anything this week, it was that geographical proximity didn't guarantee a body closeness to a person they loved.

He closed his eyes for a moment to collect himself, then carefully refolded the paper and tucked it in his pocket.

"I thank thee."

"You're welcome. But I didn't make a trip over here just to give you a timetable."

Caleb tilted his head, and Jacob leaned forward in his chair, resting his forearms on his knees.

"I haven't been able to get what Fiona said to you out of my head."

Caleb snorted. "Which part? The part where she said she couldn't marry me or the part where she said she couldn't even see me any longer?" The words were acid in his mouth, but bitterness was the only way he'd found to keep the anguish at bay.

"The part where she said you didn't know what you were asking."

"I knew precisely what I was asking her. I was asking her to be my wife." Caleb jutted out his chin.

Jacob raised a finger. "Just listen." He dropped his

hand back in his lap and scooted a little closer to Caleb. "As I said, I couldn't stop mulling it over. Something about that statement seemed so familiar, but I couldn't quite place it. Until Lyddie overheard me muttering to myself and asked me what I was going on about." He chuckled and shook his head. "She's a sharp one. Gets it from her mother." He smiled and stared off into the distance, and Caleb knew he was thinking about his late wife. Typically he indulged Jacob in these daydreams, but he hadn't the patience today.

"And?"

Jacob blinked, and his eyes refocused on Caleb. "Right. Sorry. Anyhow, before I knew what I was doing, I told Lyddie the whole story. I didn't mention your or Fiona's names, though. She probably figured it out, but I suppose it doesn't matter now. And you know what she asked me?"

Caleb began jiggling his right knee. Jacob usually got straight to the point. Why was he tormenting him now? "Clearly, I do not."

"She asked me, 'Does this woman have a job?'" Jacob leaned back in his chair and crossed his arms over his chest, smiling smugly.

Caleb creased his brow. "What has that got to do with it?"

"Don't you see?" Jacob uncrossed his arms and leaned forward again, earnest. "If she marries, she'll lose her job."

Caleb's hand flew to his throat. That had never occurred to him. Quaker women usually continued to participate in their calling after marriage and even motherhood—though they tended to work for other Friends. He'd never considered the ramifications of marriage on Fiona's career at the Smithsonian, though he should have. Fiona had told him about Nicole having to resign once she wed. He rocked back in his seat, stunned. He'd been so selfishly certain that he was offering something wonderful to Fiona that he'd never considered that marrying him would force her to sacrifice something else. It stung a little that she'd chosen her job over him, but Fiona didn't hold just *any* job. She was the director of the Smithsonian Institution Library, for pity's sake.

"If not for that lofty position she holds, I bet she would have accepted your proposal straightaway," Jacob said, that smug grin still on his face.

Jacob's words didn't bring Caleb the comfort he supposed his friend had intended.

"That's all very well and good," Caleb said, "but I fail to see how this solves my dilemma. I'm still without her, and the children still insist they won't sing on Seventh Day." He rubbed his temples. "The entire Meeting is going to be disappointed. To say nothing of the other people who were planning to attend." He'd seen the handbills all along the route between Georgetown and Capitol Hill. Alexander Clark had invited the entire city.

Jacob reached over and patted his shoulder. "Forget the concert. What you need to worry about is getting Fiona back. You're miserable without her."

Caleb looked up at his friend. "I am, but what am I to do? She can't be with me without giving up her position, and I can't ask her to make that sacrifice."

"I don't know," Jacob said. "But you have to figure out something." His eyes had gone red around the rims. "I know all too well what it's like to have to carry on without the love of my life. I'd do almost anything to have Hannah back. Believe me when I tell you to avoid living with this feeling, whatever it takes. Get on your knees and beg if you have to, but for God's sake, man, don't give up."

****

Fiona dragged herself in to work that same morning. She hadn't slept well all week. Nicole's words about deciding which path she'd regret missing more haunted her every time she closed her eyes. Because she knew the answer: Caleb. But that was the selfish answer. What of Susan's sacrifices to help her reach her current position? What of the girls like Martha who saw in her an example of what a woman could do if given the opportunity? Considering that, she didn't think she could, in good conscience, choose Caleb. Not to mention he might not be an option any longer. She wasn't sure she'd give someone another chance after they gave her the mitten the way she had.

The library also felt so cold and lonely now that she was there by herself. Martha had made Nicole's absence bearable, but now with the girl gone as well, the cavernous space felt like a mausoleum. And of course, her heartbreak and the loneliness at work weren't the only reasons she hadn't been sleeping well. There was also—

"Miss Ellicott!" Secretary Clark's voice rattled her already aching head as he strode into the library. Fiona wished she'd worn black or brown today instead of red. In a darker color, she might have been able to lean against one of the shelves and blend in with the books. Instead, she stood out like—what was the phrase she'd heard Spryly use?—a polecat in a perfume shop.

"Miss Ellicott," the secretary repeated as he reached

Fiona. His cheeks and nose were red, as if he'd just come in from outside, and Fiona could smell the cold winter air wafting off his coat. "Twenty-four hours."

"I'm sorry, sir?"

"Just over twenty-four hours until the concert tomorrow night. Just now, Vice President Breckinridge stopped me on his way to the President's House to tell me how much he and his wife are looking forward to it. They intend to bring their children. Please tell me you've convinced the orphans to perform."

Fiona gripped the edge of the nearest bookshelf to steady herself as a wave of nausea threatened the meager breakfast she'd eaten. The vice president. Lovely.

"I—I'm still working on that, sir."

Truth was, she hadn't been working very hard. She'd sent a page to the orphanage a couple of days ago with a note for Martha, pleading with the girl to change her mind, but Martha's reply had been only three short, heart-wrenching words: "I am sorry." Nicole had suggested Fiona visit the home to plead her case in person, but desperate as she was becoming, Fiona hadn't been able to force herself to go. The children knew she'd hurt Caleb, and she didn't think she could bear seeing their disapproving faces if she turned up. But it was looking increasingly likely that she'd have to pluck up the courage.

The secretary's usually kindly expression was stern, reminding Fiona of an old schoolmaster of hers whose idea of teaching was shouting fire and brimstone until his pupils were near tears.

"I certainly hope you are," he said. "The *vice president*, Miss Ellicott. The man who leads the Senate, which is one of the bodies responsible for our funding.

I'm certain I don't need to explain to you what that means for a fledgling institution such as ours."

Fiona's stomach gurgled dangerously. "No, sir. I'll work it out."

Secretary Clark nodded. "Good. Because if nothing else, donations are already pouring in for the orphanage. Piles of clothes and toys and enough books for them to open their own library."

He turned and strode out of the library, the heavy door thudding shut behind him, its echo tolling through the library like a funeral bell.

Fiona lay awake again that night, tossing and turning but knowing she'd never get to sleep. She hadn't come up with any other ideas that day and had resigned herself to traveling to Georgetown in the morning to speak with the children and Caleb directly, to beg if she had to. Maybe a mention of all the gifts awaiting them would change the children's minds. They could all use more clothes, and Spryly, especially, would be excited over the prospect of new toys. And of course, Martha would be thrilled to get her hands on all those books Secretary Clark had mentioned.

All those books.

Fiona gasped and sat bolt upright in bed.

Chapter Nineteen

The next morning, Fiona was in such a rush to get dressed that she got tangled up in her crinoline and fell to the floor of her bedroom with a crash that prompted her older niece to bang on her door and inquire about her welfare. Assuring the girl she was all right, she hurried into a day dress and raced out her bedroom door.

"Fiona!" Susan called as Fiona tore through the hall to the front door. "Where are you going in such a hurry?"

"I have to get to Georgetown!" she shouted back as she yanked open the door.

Praise be, a cab was approaching just as she scurried down the front steps to the street. She flagged down the driver and leapt into the carriage, ordering the man to get to Georgetown with all deliberate speed.

She couldn't believe she hadn't put it together sooner. All those books. Keeping the home front going. Making a difference even without being on the front lines. It had all connected in the dark of last night, as if by a visit from a Christmas ghost.

Drumming her fingers on her thigh, she peered out the carriage window at the rowhouses zipping past. Couldn't this horse go any faster?

She prayed Caleb would be receptive to her idea. Though she supposed that first he'd have to accept her apology. She should have explained things better to him last week. But surely he'd see the brilliance in this plan.

He simply had to.

They rumbled down Pennsylvania Avenue for several blocks until, just before Seventh Street, the cab driver yanked the horse to a stop that threw Fiona forward off her seat. She crashed in a heap onto the floor of the carriage.

"Good gracious!" she hollered, leaning out the window. "Whatever was that about?"

Before the driver could respond, a policeman hustled up alongside the carriage. The man was red-faced and out of breath.

"Sorry," he said to the driver between gasps, "but you'll have to take another route. Got a pack of angry hogs loose 'tween here and Twelfth Street. Been crashing through one saloon after another. Ain't safe to drive through."

If Fiona hadn't lived in Washington City for the past seven years, she never would have believed him. Unfortunately, livestock running rampant through town was all too common, though it had been some time since she'd seen it happen. But of all the days!

"How far north are you blocking off?" Fiona asked the policeman.

"All the way to Massachusetts, ma'am."

Massachusetts Avenue? Goodness! Just how large was this pack of hogs?

"Turn left!" she hollered to the driver. "Take us across the canal and down B Street. We can cut back up Fifteenth once we're past the Mall."

She settled back on her seat as the driver clucked to the horse and turned them south. The detour was going to cost them at least ten minutes. Ten more agonizing minutes. There were only eleven hours remaining until the children were due to sing at the Castle. If they weren't there to entertain Vice President Breckinridge, Secretary Clark was going to have her head. Worse still, it was delaying her making things right with Caleb.

The driver, or perhaps the horse, must have sensed her urgency, because they flew along even faster than before, the carriage jolting on the lumpy roads. She never had understood why Washington's streets were so abysmally primitive. Even with the macadam paving, they were nearly impassable most of the year. Washington City was rather swampy, but so was much of the Incan Empire, and they'd managed to create usable roads four hundred years ago.

They rattled past the Castle toward Fifteenth Street. The air from outside nipped at her nose and cheeks, but Fiona kept the window curtain pulled up so she could track their progress toward Georgetown. As the unfinished Washington Monument hove into view, they hit a particularly hard rut in the road, and Fiona bounced off her seat again, landing hard on her left knee. She rubbed it, certain she'd have a bruise by this evening.

She hauled herself back onto her seat and, in her peripheral vision, caught sight of a man running pell-mell down the sidewalk in the opposite direction, back toward the Castle. This must be the owner of the pack of angry hogs. But no, she thought, glancing at him again. He was going the wrong way. Coming from the west like he was, 'twould be faster to go up Fifteenth like she was about to and then cut east toward Seventh. Then she realized there was something very familiar about the man's short-crowned black hat and the simple cut of his coat. Heart pounding, she leaned out the window and hollered to the driver to stop.

****

The cold, fetid air was razor sharp, and it sliced Caleb's lungs with every breath as he charged down B Street behind the Castle. His only saving grace was that the city hadn't yet gotten any snow or ice to slip on. He hadn't slept a wink last night, and his head was as foggy as Dickens's London. He'd lain awake all night trying to devise something to say to Fiona, something that acknowledged her dilemma yet still pled his case. Even after agonizing over it for eight hours, he had nothing. But Jacob was right. He couldn't simply let her go. He had to say *something* to her, even if it was merely to tell her he loved her one last time.

And if he'd known he'd have to take a detour getting to Capitol Hill, he would have scrounged up the money for a cab. He'd gotten all the way to Tenth Street only to be stopped by a policeman who made him turn back. He'd had to backtrack five blocks to Fifteenth, cross the canal, and head down the Mall, trying not to think about his last trek down this path when Fiona had said she couldn't marry him.

He'd made the journey from Georgetown to Fiona's home in Capitol Hill by foot several times, but never at full speed, and his diversion had added an extra mile to the trip. There was a good chance he might collapse on the Mall and die staring up at the scrim of gray clouds hanging heavily in the sky, but he kept running. If he reached Fiona's house and she'd already set out somewhere for the day, he'd die anyway. His mind raced while his legs kept churning. Just past the Mall, he'd turn onto Sixth Street and cut onto Maryland Avenue. That would take him back across the canal and right up to the Capitol Building, not far from Fiona's house. Surely the angry hogs wouldn't have made it that far.

Just as he reached the east edge of the Castle, he thought he heard someone holler his name, barely audible over his ragged breathing. He shook it off and kept running, though despite his desperation to reach Fiona's house, his body was slowing to a jog. He heard the shout again. It was undeniably his name, but how could that be? He didn't know anyone on this end of town. Well, no one except—

Fiona.

He stopped dead and spun on the spot, his eyes darting wildly, trying to find her. There. On the sidewalk, in that light gray dress with the pink and yellow flowers that he loved so much. When she noticed that he'd spotted her, she waved frantically and called his name again. He'd never heard a more beautiful sound in all his life. She was nearly all the way at the opposite end of the Castle, and he briefly marveled at how loudly she could yell—especially for someone who spent her days in a library—before he sucked in a searing, rattling breath and took off running toward her. His legs were two sticks of smoldering iron, but he forced them to full speed. Fiona had told him once that the Castle was 453 feet long. He wasn't sure why he remembered that, but surely he could make it that much farther.

Fiona aided him by covering part of the distance, probably as fast as she could in her heavy skirts. They reached each other halfway, just in front of the South Tower, the square fortification looming over them. Fiona's cheeks were flushed, and the tip of her nose was pink, as if she'd been out in the chilly, gray morning for at least several minutes herself. She was more beautiful than ever, and Caleb wanted to take her in his arms and kiss her until he was breathless.

Though he already *was* breathless. So much so that he couldn't even say hello. He bent over, braced his hands on his knees, and gulped in lungfuls of the frosty air until his throat and chest screamed. Fiona rubbed his back, and he thought that if he was going to suffocate right here in front of the Smithsonian, at least he'd die happy.

"Did you run the entire way from Georgetown?" Fiona said, surprise ringing in her voice.

Still gasping, Caleb nodded, hoping she'd never stop caressing his back. "Woulda been...thy house...already...but..."

"There was a pack of hogs running amok, I know. Isn't Washington City simply lovely?"

He looked up and saw Fiona smiling down at him, a genuine smile that reached her eyes. And he realized he'd been wrong a moment ago. *Now* she was more beautiful than ever. Chest still heaving, he straightened and took her hands in his.

"Fiona." He paused to suck in another breath. "I've come to understand why thee had to reject my proposal. Please accept my deepest apologies. I hadn't considered that marriage would cost thee thy career."

Fiona's face crumpled and her eyes filled. She shook her head. "I'm the one who should be sorry. I owed you a full explanation that night, but I lost my nerve." She looked away, toward the Castle. "It seemed so selfish to turn you down for my job."

Caleb laid one hand on her cheek and turned her face back toward him. "Not selfish at all. Thee has worked so hard and is in such an enviable position."

Fiona blinked hard, and Caleb could tell she was

barely holding back the tears welled in her eyes. "That day in the lecture room, when you asked me my thoughts on marriage...I truly thought there was a chance Secretary Clark might let me continue on after marrying. But then he said how glad he was that he didn't have to worry about me losing my head and leaving the Smithsonian for a man, and..."

A tickle of hope fluttered deep in Caleb's gut. "Wait. Did thee *want* to marry me?"

"Of course I did." A rogue tear broke free from Fiona's left eye and coursed down her cheek. "I *do*." She looked away again. "Though I don't expect you'd ever have me now."

Caleb rocked back on his heels. Have her? Was she mad? "Fiona," he said, wiping the tear from her cheek, "there's nothing I want more than thee."

The fluttering in his stomach grew to a cyclone in the agonizing seconds it took Fiona to turn her head back to him. A smile spread slowly across her face, and she took hold of his hands again.

"In that case, Caleb Fox," she said, her voice quivering, "since the Friends believe in the equality of women, I feel justified in asking *you* this time." The corners of her mouth turned up in that coy smile he adored. "Would you do me the great honor of marrying me?"

A bubble of laughter sprang from deep in Caleb's chest. With a hoot of joy, he wrapped his arms around Fiona's waist and spun her in a circle before pressing his lips to hers. She pressed back against him, deepening the kiss, and he lingered there, relishing the sensation he thought he'd never feel again. Only when a passerby made a lewd comment did he let her go. She laughed and touched her gloved fingertips to her swollen lips.

"Is that a yes, then?" she asked.

He pressed his forehead to hers. "'Tis. But Fiona…" Biting the inside of his cheek, he took a step back. "What about all this?" He swept a hand toward the Castle, the solid, red sentinel keeping watch over the Mall. "What about thy career?"

Fiona smiled. "I may have to give up the Smithsonian, but I think I've devised a plan to keep my career." She popped up on her toes and whispered into his ear, and Caleb felt the joy slowly flow back into his core, along with a mixture of awe and admiration at the extent of her plan.

"Thee is certain this is what thee wants?" His eyes searched hers, looking for any crack in the certainty there.

"'Tis." She caressed his cheek. "Besides, what is librarianship but collecting and disseminating knowledge to people? I don't need a castle to do that."

A tear slid down Caleb's cheek, warming his skin with a glow he felt spread through his whole body. "Then, Fiona Ellicott, as it is Christmas Eve, shall we go home and share this wonderful gift with our children?"

Fiona gazed at him through her own tear-filled eyes. "Yes, please."

That evening, Fiona sat next to Caleb in the Smithsonian lecture room, listening to the children sing more beautifully than she'd heard them do in any rehearsal. They'd all shrieked with joy when she arrived at the home on Caleb's arm that morning and told them the good news.

"Does this mean the concert's back on?" Patricia asked.

"It is if you want it to be," Fiona said.

The children immediately agreed to sing, though Martha worked up a lather, panicking because they hadn't rehearsed all week.

"You act like we're dumber than rocks," Spryly said. Then he threw back his head and sang, "God rest ye merry, Wenceslas, may nothing Tannenbaum!" He grinned at Martha's stricken expression. "See? Ain't forgotten nothin'."

Now, Fiona glanced around at the audience. So many people had arrived for the concert that even the standing room was full. Downstairs in the lobby, gifts for the orphanage were piled high, including the stacks and stacks of books Secretary Clark had mentioned. Fiona smiled. She'd certainly have her work cut out for her, organizing all those books into the Friends' Home School's new library. She suspected those books, plus the ones she could purchase with some of the donations now pouring in for the orphanage, would soon overflow their current space. She and Caleb had discussed finding a larger building for the home in the coming years. They'd need it if they hoped to not only take in more orphans but also to open a school that any child in the area could attend. Likely, they'd need separate buildings for the school and the orphans' housing.

She glanced over to where Vice President Breckinridge and his wife sat toward the end of the row. The vice president beamed with joy as the children sang "O Tannenbaum," and Fiona suspected she'd be able to persuade him to lend some assistance in funding their school. Next to the Breckinridges sat Senator William Seward with his wife and daughter. They were clearly enjoying the performance, too, young Fanny Seward mouthing along silently to the lyrics. Fiona knew there was no love lost between Breckinridge and Seward, but if two men from clashing political parties could sit next to one another and enjoy a few carols, perhaps there was still hope for the nation at large.

She flicked her gaze to Caleb and caught his eye. He smiled and gave her a swift, chaste peck on the cheek. She had a difficult conversation with Secretary Clark ahead of her on Monday, but at least for tonight she would sit next to the man she loved and listen to their children charm the city. She intertwined her fingers with Caleb's and gently squeezed his hand because tonight, everything was perfect. How could it not be, when she was celebrating Christmas in a castle?

Epilogue

(Almost) One Year Later
December 19, 1860

Caleb shivered as a blast of frigid air blew him into the house. He smiled to hear the happy shouts of the children playing games upstairs. The house had been a touch quieter in the year since Spryly moved to California, but not by as much as he'd expected. He peeled off his coat, hat, scarf, and gloves, and stepped into the parlor, where Fiona was organizing books on one of the many shelves they'd erected there since last Christmas. She must not have heard him come in because she didn't turn around, so he said her name.

She turned, and when she saw him, her face lit with joy. She set down the books she was shelving and scurried over to kiss him.

"And how are we this afternoon?" he asked, laying his hands lovingly on her swollen belly. They both laughed when the baby kicked hard. Jacob had said they probably had only another week or two before the little one made its arrival.

"Happy you're home, apparently." She kissed him again. "How was the post office?"

He grinned and whipped an envelope from his pocket with a grand flourish. Fiona's eyes popped wide.

"Is that from Spryly?"

He grinned. "'Tis."

"What's it say?"

He chuckled as she tried to snatch the letter from his hand.

"I've not read it yet either," he said, holding the letter above his head, out of her reach. "Settle thyself in a chair and I'll read it aloud."

Fiona dropped heavily into one of the armchairs near the fire, and Caleb took the other chair, opening the envelope as he sat. He first pulled out a note from William Carter's second son, Frank, saying that he'd transcribed the letter for Spryly and warning that he'd been commanded to transcribe it verbatim. Caleb smiled. Spryly had always detested his writing lessons because, as he said, his brain thought faster than his hand could scribble. Caleb set the note aside and extracted the letter.

Lucky Star Ranch
Placerville, Calif.
November 15, 1860
Dear Caleb and Fiona,

I guess by now you're about to have another one of them Christmas concerts at the Castle. I'm sure sorry I can't be there, but I ain't sorry I'm not in Washington no more. It stinks a lot less out here. But I do miss those mummies. I'm glad you're still taking everyone to the Castle to see them. Next time you're there, tell them Spryly says hello.

Fiona laughed. "I'll be sure to do that on Seventh Day. If Secretary Clark hasn't already been doing it himself. Last time I saw him, he mentioned how much he misses seeing Spryly at the museum."

Caleb smiled, grateful that Fiona and Secretary Clark had parted on amicable terms. He suspected the success of the children's concert last year helped. It had barely concluded when the secretary approached him about repeating the performance. Martha had been rehearsing with the children since mid-October so they'd have a few more songs to sing this year.

I got a letter from Martha saying how much she likes being the new assistant over at the library there. It was awful nice of Secretary Clark to hire her and let Fiona stay on long enough after you all got hitched to train her good. I bet that new librarian ain't doing half as good a job as Fiona.

Pa says I'm supposed to tell you all congratulations on buying that building to set up your school and library. So, congratulations on the new school and library. I wish I could see it, but I'm sure the other kids will like it a lot more than I would have anyhow.

Caleb had to pause his reading to laugh at this understatement. He couldn't imagine any place Spryly would have enjoyed being at less than the new school. But Spryly was right about the other children's excitement, and it was thanks to their performance that Caleb and Fiona's Meeting had been able to purchase the new building.

The concert had brought in nearly a thousand dollars in donations last Christmas, and several wealthy Washingtonians with philanthropic tendencies had continued to contribute to the home in the following months. Holding another concert at the end of this week was largely a thank-you to Washington City.

Anyhow, you got to send word the minute the baby arrives and make sure you tell her all about her big brother Spryly out in California. Or him, if it's a boy. Frank and I been taking bets on what it's gonna be, and if you all have a girl, he owes me a whole dime's worth of gumdrops. So try to have a girl, all right?

In Friendship,

Spryly Carter

Caleb closed his eyes. The closing of Spryly's letter was so beautifully Quaker, but the boy was gambling again. He wasn't sure whether to laugh or groan. Fiona made the decision for him by laughing heartily.

"Sounds like Will has his hands full. Spryly really is the Artful Dodger."

Caleb grinned. Fiona's joy was too infectious for him to be sour over a candy wager. "That he is. But I'm sure Will can handle it. He's managed Frank for this long, and to hear Jacob tell it, Frank's as ornery as Spryly." He stood and kissed Fiona's forehead. "And speaking of Dickens, I think I'll start reading *A Christmas Carol* to everyone before bed tonight."

Fiona caressed his cheek. "That sounds lovely. I'll make a big pot of drinking chocolate for us all to enjoy while you read."

Caleb stared at his wife, a tangible reminder of how quickly life could change. While at the post office, he'd heard a group of other men debating loudly whether the southern states would secede from the Union soon, and he worried they might be on the brink of another momentous change.

But if working with orphans—especially Spryly— had taught him anything, it was to live in the moment, to enjoy the happy moments as they came. So, he would hold his country in the Light, and at least for tonight, he would bask contentedly in the love of his wife and the children they loved as their own.

And perhaps the spirit of the season would turn his

countrymen's hearts like the Christmas spirits had turned Ebenezer Scrooge's. It could happen.

Because what was Christmas if not a season of hope?

Author's Note

Washington, DC, in the nineteenth century was a dump. "Cesspool" is actually a better term, and I don't mean that metaphorically. Situated at the lowest point of a large drainage basin, the area was originally marshy swampland. Even after development, the downtown area often flooded, and only the poorest of the poor took up residence in the most flood-prone areas, such as around the White House.

Making matters worse, city planners built a canal along the north side of the National Mall, which was much smaller then than it is now. Hoping to make Washington City (as it was called until 1871) a shipping port, the canal connected the Potomac River to both the Anacostia River and Tiber Creek. Opened in 1815, the canal was too shallow to handle the tide coming in from the Anacostia River and frequently overflowed. It fell into disuse by the late 1850s when this story takes place, and by the time of the Civil War was nothing more than an open-air sewer cutting through the heart of the city. Its stench and tendency to breed diseases such as malaria, yellow fever, and cholera led city planners to cover it over, beginning in 1871. The canal continues to flow today, safely paved over by Constitution Avenue NW.

The city was dangerous too. Crime gangs and half-feral livestock roamed the streets, which were often covered in several inches of sticky mud. The skimpy police force had no hope of maintaining order, and dueling was common. Saloons and brothels mushroomed to meet the demands of the politicians.

Out of this swampy, crime- and disease-riddled pit rose what would become the largest museum, education, and research complex in the world. Founded in 1846, the Smithsonian Institution's first building, lovingly dubbed "the Castle" for its medieval architectural style, opened in 1855. It originally housed a library, a lecture hall, several exhibit rooms, and the living quarters for the Secretary of the

Smithsonian. Following a devastating fire in 1865 that destroyed the lecture hall where the children in the story perform their concert, many of the exhibits, along with the library, were moved to other facilities. Today, the Smithsonian comprises twenty-one museums, the National Zoo, and nine research facilities. The library is no longer a single building but rather twenty-one research libraries that support the museums and research facilities. The Castle is now mostly used for administration, though the West Wing where the fictional Fiona Ellicott worked is a quiet place for visitors to rest.

Fiona Ellicott, named for Andrew Ellicott, who was the lead surveyor of Washington, DC, is fictional, but she is inspired by Jane Wadden Turner, who was the first paid female employee of the Smithsonian. Like Fiona, Turner's parents both died by the time she was ten, leaving her in the care of her older sister. Turner's older brother, William, assumed command of the Smithsonian library in 1857 and placed Turner in charge of creating the catalogue. When William died in 1859, the real secretary of the Smithsonian at the time, Joseph Henry (who really did complain about the stench wafting up into his living quarters) placed Turner in charge of the library. Though she never held a position in which she supervised men, she worked for the Smithsonian until her retirement in 1887, living long enough to see the library amass the world-class collection Fiona dreams of in this story.

Turner never married, so we can't say whether marriage would have cost her the position at the Smithsonian, but well into the twentieth century, society frowned on married women working in a profession. It's entirely likely that, had Turner married, she would have had to leave the Smithsonian.

As a member of the Religious Society of Friends ("Quakers"), Caleb Fox—named for the Friends' founder, George Fox—would have stuck out in Washington City too. Though well known in Pennsylvania, Quakers in other places were often deemed odd for their plain style of dressing and their use of the "plain speech" described in my note at the beginning of the book. Originally quite insular, the Quakers, like many American religious groups, were beginning to loosen up by the mid-nineteenth century. While they certainly would have encouraged one of their own to marry a fellow Friend, marriage to non-Friends was no longer such a scandal, especially if the non-Friend showed interest in joining the Meeting.

While there was a Quaker meetinghouse on Massachusetts Avenue in 1859, there was not, to my knowledge, a Quaker orphanage in Georgetown (which was a separate city until it merged with Washington in 1871). Sadly, the area was slow to address the plight of homeless and parentless children, not providing any support for them until 1863, when a newsboys' home opened. It was soon reorganized into the Industrial Home School, which was my model for the Friends' Home School in this story. Originally situated at the corner that is now 7th Street and Independence Avenue NW (many street names have changed since 1859), a larger building opened in Georgetown, where the school eventually absorbed the old Poor and Work House of Georgetown as well. The Industrial Home School provided housing and education to thousands of destitute children until it closed in 1954.

Caleb Fox and his fellow Quakers weren't the only Americans in 1859 who'd never celebrated Christmas. For much of American history, most Christian groups shunned— if not outright outlawed—the celebration of Christmas because of its connection to the pagan celebration of Saturnalia. The Puritans and, later, the Presbyterians, were some of the longest holdouts. While the Quakers had their own reasons for not celebrating, as mentioned in the story, they were slow to pick up on the holiday as well. Though Christmas trees didn't become common in non-German American households until a few years after this story is set, the holiday itself was quickly gaining ground. The orphans' Christmas concert at the Smithsonian is entirely a product of my imagination, but carols and gift-giving were common by 1859, thanks in no small part to the publication of Charles Dickens's *A Christmas Carol* in 1843.

History buffs will note that the epilogue takes place the day before South Carolina seceded from the United States, kicking off the "Secession Winter" that would lead to the Civil War's outbreak the following April. I imagine Caleb and Fiona would have had their hands full during the war years and immediately after, caring for all the children orphaned by that horrific conflict. But I also imagine they never would have given up hope that things would improve, that the Light of the Divine within us all would eventually shine through.

And so, in the words of Charles Dickens, "God bless us, Every One!"

Recommended Reading

Dickey, J.D. 2015. *Empire of Mud: The Secret History of Washington, DC*. Guilford, CT: Lyons Press.

Hamm, Thomas D. 2003. *The Quakers in America*. New York: Columbia University Press.

Restad, Penne L. 1995. *Christmas in America: A History*. New York: Oxford University Press.

Stamm, Richard E. 2012. *The Castle: An Illustrated History of the Smithsonian Building*. 2nd ed. Washington, DC: Smithsonian Institution.

~*~

ACKNOWLEDGEMENTS

As always, I could not have written this book without the unwavering support of my husband, Dan. Thank you for listening to me ramble about nineteenth-century Washington, DC, and for putting up with that giant 1856 street map that spent several months spread across the dining room table. I love you so much.

Thanks of course to Mom, Dad, Charissa, the aunts and uncles, and the cousin squad for cheering me on and being eager to read my little stories.

To my critique partners, Emily DeBorde, Kristin Durfee, and Jennifer Leigh Pezzano, your feedback was invaluable, and I owe you all big time.

Finally, a special thanks to my friends (and Friends!) at the Winter Park Friends Meeting. Your support, guidance, love, and deviled eggs over the past couple of years have touched me immeasurably.

A word about the author…

Sarah Hendess is an editor, runner, and cross-stitcher who grew up in Hutchinson, KS, and Pittsburgh, PA. She now lives in Lake Mary, FL, with her husband, son, two cats, two dogs, and a 23-year-old turtle.

Follow her on Facebook at:
 http://www.facebook.com/sarahhendessauthor
Follow her on Instagram at:
@thewritehendess

Thank you for purchasing
this publication of The Wild Rose Press, Inc.

For questions or more information
contact us at
info@thewildrosepress.com.

The Wild Rose Press, Inc.

9 781509 256457